*A Candlelight
Ecstasy Romance*®

**"WHAT DIFFERENCE DOES IT MAKE THAT I
KNEW YOU WERE MASQUERADING AS A SO-
PHISTICATED NEW YORK INTERIOR DESIGNER
ALL ALONG? I'M IN LOVE WITH YOU, LIZZIE!"
MICHAEL CRIED.**

"You don't understand. I became Elisabeth Guest because I didn't *want* your help. I didn't want to be
patronized. I wanted you to hire me because of my
talent, not because you felt sorry for a girl from your
hometown."

"I never felt sorry for you, Lizzie," Michael said
softly.

"You signed the contract practically without looking
at it. You hardly even looked at the space plans. You let
me lie and suffer from guilt about pretending to be
someone I'm not while you laughed. And last night. . ."

"Do you want me to forget that last night ever happened? Would that make you feel better? Well, I can't.
I won't!"

CANDLELIGHT ECSTASY ROMANCES®

INTERIOR DESIGNS

Carla Neggers

A CANDLELIGHT ECSTASY ROMANCE®

Published by
Dell Publishing Co., Inc.
1 Dag Hammarskjold Plaza
New York, New York 10017

ISBN: 0-440-14119-2

Printed in the United States of America

First printing—August 1985

To Our Readers:

We have been delighted with your enthusiastic response to Candlelight Ecstasy Romances®, and we thank you for the interest you have shown in this exciting series.

In the upcoming months we will continue to present the distinctive, sensuous love stories you have come to expect only from Ecstasy. We look forward to bringing you many more books from your favorite authors, and also the very finest work from new authors of contemporary romantic fiction.

As always we are striving to present the unique, absorbing love stories that you enjoy most—books that are more than ordinary romance.

Your suggestions and comments are always welcome. Please write to us at the address below.

Sincerely,

The Editors
Candlelight Romances
1 Dag Hammarskjold Plaza
New York, New York 10017

CHAPTER ONE

Michael Wolfe was in his usual Monday morning foul mood when he opened the door to his office and saw the woman standing on his desk. She had three plastic tape measures around her neck and a yardstick pressed up against his ceiling. Wolfe was too surprised even to growl, so he just stood there in the doorway, staring.

The woman was too busy measuring to notice him. She had a pencil stuck behind her ear and a scrap of paper between her lips. Wolfe thought she was one hell of a sight: paint-bespeckled engineer pants and NYU sweatshirt; bright blue polka-dotted bandana tied around a head of wispy, fire-red curls; bright red boys' sneakers on what appeared to be tiny feet.

What enraged Wolfe most was that the woman's tiny feet were planted firmly in the middle of his very expensive slate blotter.

Wolfe started to cringe, but the woman shifted slightly, stretching up higher to mark one end of the yardstick with her index finger and then moving the yardstick

7

across the ceiling. She lifted her left foot off the blotter and balanced on the toes of her right foot. If she fell, she would come crashing down on his dusty, but original, pewter sculpture. He wasn't quite sure what the thing was, but the client who had given it to him for Christmas one year had assured Wolfe that it was a very modern and very valuable work by an up-and-coming sculptor. But now Wolfe couldn't have cared less if it was a Dégas as he noticed the woman's paint-bespeckled engineer pants stretched over the curve of her hips. She had nice, slim hips and a lovely, rounded derriere. Wolfe's mood began to improve.

He folded his arms over his chest and cleared his throat, quietly announcing his presence.

Holding the yardstick in place, she peered under her outstretched arm and saw him. Her pale cornflower-blue eyes widened. He leaned against the doorjamb and smiled, not showing any teeth. Even from a distance of seven feet he could see the sprinkle of golden freckles across her pert nose. He gathered that she was surprised to see him, which suited him just fine. He liked to have the element of surprise working on his behalf.

She brought one hand down, plucked the scrap of paper from between her lips, and, to Wolfe's surprise, broke into a dazzling smile. "Hi," she said cheerily. "I'll be out of your way in two secs."

"Why are you measuring my ceiling?" he asked, his arms still folded.

"Huh?" she said.

"My ceiling," he repeated. "Why are you measuring it?"

She frowned down at him and then said, as if to an idiot, "Because it's easier to get the dimensions of the room that way. I didn't want to have to move a lot of furniture around."

"I see."

He thought he sounded sarcastic, and even arrogant, because, of course, he didn't see at all, but she gave him another dazzling smile, said, "That's good," and turned her attention back to taking measurements.

Wolfe gave up. Without another word he went back into the outer office, closing the door hard behind him. He stopped short of slamming it: he didn't want to startle the woman and end up having to peel her off that hunk of pewter.

Gwen Duprey smiled knowingly. She was Wolfe's long-suffering secretary, a fifty-year-old woman who could have run the Ottoman Empire on an eight-hour day, with forty-five minutes off for lunch. "I tried to warn you," she said.

Wolfe glared at her. "Gwen, there's a woman standing on my desk, measuring my ceiling."

"Yes, I know."

He huffed, recalling his somewhat abrupt arrival less than ten minutes earlier. Gwen could have tried to tell him the sky was falling, and he wouldn't have paid any attention. Mondays. It wasn't so much that he hated them as it was that he hated weekends, especially long, quiet ones. The hell with it, he thought, aggravated again, and he jerked a thumb toward his office. "Who is she?" he demanded.

9

"I don't recall her name." Gwen licked a stamp, unperturbed. "Meg would know—"

Wolfe turned purple. "*Oakes!*" he bellowed. "Get out here!"

Gwen pressed the stamp onto an envelope and calmly answered the phone, which rang incessantly at the offices of Wolfe's high-powered New York literary agency.

Meg Oakes strode into the outer office and politely asked what was up. Wolfe glowered at her. Six months she'd been working for him, and he hadn't managed to intimidate her for more than two seconds running—if that. This both satisfied and irritated him. But, since she'd just married one of his top clients, he figured he was stuck with her. He'd already lost Jonathan Mc-Gavock, also known as famous thriller writer Ross Greening, once, and he was damned if he was going to lose him again by firing his unflappable wife! Wolfe was only blustering, though. He knew better than anyone that Meg Oakes was a damned good agent and possibly the best of his three associates.

But that did *not* explain the woman standing on his desk.

Wolfe nodded toward his office. "Who is she?"

Meg looked blank. Since marrying a forester/writer, she'd taken up wearing chamois shirts and argyle socks on days she didn't have to go out of the office. Wolfe had made a mental note that if she showed up in a coonskin hat, he'd have to have a few words with her, but chamois shirts he could live with. Today's was maroon. "Who's who?" she asked.

"The redhead standing on my desk!"

10

"Redhead standing on—I can't imagine . . . oh! That must be your designer!"

"My what?" Wolfe snapped.

"Elisabeth . . . I don't know, Elisabeth Somebody-or-other. I don't remember her name. But she's a brunette, not a redhead."

"I'm not color-blind, Oakes, and what the hell are you talking about?"

"She stopped by Friday while you were out. Oh, yes, her name is Elisabeth Guest. She arranged to come in today to take measurements. She didn't want to disturb you, so I said this morning would be best. I gather she sent an assistant. I assumed you knew."

"How could I know? I've never heard of the woman before!"

Meg gave him a dubious look. "But you hired her."

Wolfe grunted. "I did no such thing. Is this your idea, Oakes?"

"Certainly not. I'd never go over your head and arrange to have your offices redecorated and—"

"*What!*"

"Wolfe, really," Meg said reprovingly. "Surely you wouldn't forget something like this. You gripe about us using a few extra stamps, and here you're spending thousands of dollars to redecorate and you don't even remember who you hired."

"Thousands . . ." Wolfe caught his breath, pushed back the tails of his gray cashmere coat, and stuffed his hands in his pockets. He was preparing for war. He said distinctly, "I did not hire anyone to redecorate."

11

He expected Meg to take his word for it, but she didn't. "You did too."

"Oakes . . ."

"Do you think I would let just anyone into your office? She showed me the letter you wrote her; she even gave me a copy. Would you like to see it?"

"You're damned right I would!" He turned to his secretary and thumped her perfectly good twenty-five-year-old desk. "If that woman tries to leave, you raise hell."

"I'll be sure to notify you, Mr. Wolfe," Gwen said, always the cool professional.

Wolfe led the way to Meg's office. Despite his mood he moved with his usual grace and style. He was neither tall, burly, nor particularly handsome, but that had never once bothered him. His hair had turned pure white before his thirty-fifth birthday. He liked it that way. White hair and a young face had a certain impact on people. And instead of the bruising muscle of a football player, he had the wiry, agile leanness of a squash player. Fit as a fiddle, he always said, and as intimidating as hell; that was what he was.

Meg handed him a copy of his ebony-on-ecru one-hundred-percent cotton rag stationery. "It's even your signature," she said.

Wolfe frowned and read. The letter was brief and to the point; his always were. It was to a certain Elisabeth Guest of West Seventy-second Street, New York, New York, authorizing her to redecorate the five-room office suite of Michael Wolfe Associates for a sum of money that nearly made him choke. He had lots of money, but he hated to spend it.

And the signature at the bottom *was* his.

"Either I'm going out of my mind, which I'm not," Wolfe said, "or this is a forgery."

"But how?" Meg asked. "Look, if you're trying to save face with your employees, don't bother. We might welcome pay raises more than new paint on the walls, but the place could use redecorating—"

"Mr. Wolfe!" Gwen Duprey appeared in Meg's doorway, red-faced and breathing hard. "She wouldn't listen . . . I couldn't stop her . . . I'm sorry."

Wolfe threw down the letter. "Out of my way!"

But he was too late. By the time he raced out into the hall, the redheaded woman had vanished. Just for form's sake he took the elevator down to the lobby and looked around outside, but she was gone. He growled and rode the elevator back up to his office. There was something about the unknown woman . . .

No, he thought, there probably wasn't. He knew thousands of people. And yet—was it the strands of red hair? He knew lots of redheads too. Too damned many, as a matter of fact. The dazzling smile, then? He knew lots of women with dazzling smiles too.

Meg and Gwen were waiting breathlessly in the reception area, but Wolfe just shook his head curtly. "Oakes," he said, "take a ride over to West Seventy-second and see if our Ms. Guest does happen to live there. If she does, sit on her and call me. Gwen, my office. I want you to go through everything. If anything's missing or if that woman so much as breathed on anything, I want to know about it. Questions?"

13

Gwen was shocked. "You don't think that nice woman was a thief, do you?"

"No," he said, "a spy."

"Oh, Mr. Wolfe!"

Meg scoffed. "Aren't you carrying this a bit far, Wolfe? All right, have it your way. Where will you be?"

"Luncheon appointment."

Only funerals and an occasional wedding interrupted Wolfe's maniacal schedule. Redheaded women in blue-polka-dotted bandanas found standing on his desk did not . . . even if they were spies.

Lizzie Olson leaped into a cab just as Michael Wolfe bounded out of the building. His hair was flying. Even as she gulped, yanked the door shut, and ducked, Lizzie could tell he was raging. And she knew exactly why.

"Hotel Empire," she yelled to the driver, "across from Lincoln Center—*hurry!*"

"Gotcha, lady."

The cab screeched away from the curb, catapulting Lizzie over onto her elbow, which prompted her to remember one of the primary rules of New York City living: If you value your life, never tell a cabbie to hurry.

But she figured nothing—*nothing*—could be as hair-raising as those horrible moments she'd spent in the clutches of Michael Wolfe. There he'd stood, lean, so-phisticated, *suspicious*. And there she'd stood, this side of skinny, redheaded, *caught*. She had nearly died. If he had stayed another second, she might just have thrown herself out of his seventh-story window and

14

taken her chances. Lizzie firmly believed that there were fates worse than death, and Michael Wolfe obviously was one of them.

Not that she had expected him to be. That wasn't part of her carefully plotted, wholly justifiable, if somewhat outlandish, plan. According to the plan Michael Wolfe was to have been a literary agent of considerable wealth but of dubious ethics and even more dubious taste; in short, a man in desperate need of the services of a polished, talented interior designer like herself. That was the one thing she had counted on, the constant on which she had based everything else. She and Michael Wolfe had grown up in the same small town in Kansas. She knew what he was like. And he wasn't like the man she had met today!

Lizzie moaned softly. What had seemed so simple was getting more complicated by the minute. All she had wanted to do was to come to New York, put the past behind her, and begin again. But now she needed to get her foot in the door. It was Michael's own mother, Mabel, who had suggested him and who had understood Lizzie's reluctance to ask for his help or anyone else's. But Mabel knew, and eventually Lizzie agreed, that if she designed the offices of a high-powered, well-known literary agent and did the job well, she would have her fresh start. The only problem was to get Michael to hire her.

Although neither Mabel nor Lizzie acknowledged aloud that what Lizzie needed to do was to con Michael into letting her go to work for him, the plan took shape nevertheless. Mabel said her son could afford a top

New York designer, so Lizzie might as well pretend to be one. Lizzie had come up with the name Elisabeth Guest and the idea about the letter, and Mabel had come up with the sheet of Michael's stationery.

Lizzie had known that if she told Michael that she was Lizzie Olson from Wichita, he wouldn't pay her, much less hire her. She and Michael had never been the best of friends growing up.

So, she wasn't really Elisabeth Guest, and she wasn't really a New York designer. And she resided at the Hotel Empire, not in a nice West Side apartment. It was good lodging, moderately priced (by New York standards!), and didn't require two months' rent for a security deposit or one month's rent (sometimes more!) for a realtor's fee. She had a nice, cozy little room overlooking Lincoln Center that would do just fine, at least for now. She'd go apartment hunting after she'd concluded her business with Michael Wolfe.

If she lived that long . . .

"Lady, you gonna ride on the floor the whole way?"

"No, no," she said, climbing onto the worn seat and wondering why she was permitting herself to be reduced to a babbling hick by a cabdriver. "Just a little motion sickness."

He did not reply. She already felt a bit pale and, watching the cab, which carried her one and only body, speed through a light just after it had turned red wasn't helping. She tucked a red lock inside her bright blue bandana. That was another problem: Elisabeth Guest, whom Lizzie was purporting to be, was a brunette. Michael Wolfe had just seen a redhead.

16

Hanging onto the armrest, Lizzie watched Manhattan glide by. It was a magnificent city, absolutely perfect. She loved the gray and the concrete, the unexpected touches of light and color, the potholes, the diversity, the people, the noise. She peered out the cab window, noticing everything.

But her heart was beating fiercely. It had been a close call, too close, and she'd only just begun. There was still time to rebound from her mistake, but another could ruin her. Michael Wolfe would find her out and she would return to Wichita in worse ignominy than when she had left. She'd never have her chance at making it in Manhattan.

But the Michael Wolfe whom she had just met wasn't the Michael Wolfe she had expected. Not at *all*. That Michael Wolfe she could have handled with ease. This one, she didn't know.

"Where did he get that white hair?" she mumbled to herself, and sighed.

Already he was playing havoc with her. She should never have appeared in his office dressed as herself, Lizzie Olson with the flaming-red hair and a penchant for engineer pants. When his secretary had told her Wolfe wasn't supposed to come in this morning, she'd decided to show up as herself and let Wolfe's secretary and associates think she was Elisabeth Guest's eccentric assistant. The urbane New York designer Lizzie had created would never do her own measurements.

But now she didn't know what to do. Wolfe had seen her! Curse her red hair! She'd tried to hide it under the bright-blue polka-dotted bandana, but, of course, it hadn't stayed.

17

Elisabeth Guest was not a redhead. *Lizzie Olson* was a redhead. Would Michael recognize her? If he questioned her about the resemblance between her and the red-haired woman he'd found standing on his desk this morning, she'd just coolly explain that the redhead was her cousin who was working as her assistant. But then a horrible thought seized her. Inevitably during the job—*if* she got the job—she would need to have an assistant again, and she certainly couldn't keep masquerading as two different people. One was difficult enough! Miraculously a solution presented itself to her.

"Chelsea!" she yelled.

The cabdriver cocked his head around. "Thought you said the Empire," he barked. "What is it, lady?"

"No, no, you're right. I was just—" She smiled. "You're right."

He grunted and turned his attention back to the flow of city traffic.

Chelsea Barnard was Lizzie's answer. She could be Elisabeth Guest's redheaded assistant! Of course, Chelsea was *Lizzie's* part-time assistant and best friend back in Wichita, and had hair the color of the silk on an unripened ear of corn and didn't want to come to New York, but those were just details.

"This is all getting very confusing," Lizzie said to herself, and sighed again.

At the heart of the confusion, she knew, was Michael Wolfe himself. The Michael Wolfe she had known so long ago had extremely few redeeming qualities. His parents were nice—Lizzie adored Mabel and Harold Wolfe—but Michael was another story altogether. To

18

be truthful she thought him uncharming: loudmouthed; egotistical; greedy; determined to set the whole world on fire.

And dark-haired.

"And a bad dresser," she said aloud, prompting her cabdriver to give her yet another peculiar look.

But that was all years ago, and people did change. Golly, she thought, she certainly had! But Michael had always seemed such a rock. Oh, sure, she knew he'd gone to New York and made a success of himself representing famous writers, but somehow she'd expected the Michael Wolfe she'd known and not loved fifteen years ago to be . . . well, the same! She'd expected red shoes and ribbed polyester, not cashmere and leather. She'd expected a paunch and maybe a receding hairline, not a lean, sinewy figure and that head of white hair. She'd expected Michael Wolfe to be a totally different man.

Lizzie sighed again, deeply this time. Could she admit it even to herself?

Michael Wolfe had become a rakish and sophisticated and not at all the sort of man she would want to try to con . . . for whatever reasons and however honorably.

If only his mother had warned her!

"But she did," Lizzie muttered. "You just didn't pay any attention."

Because, of course, everyone in their particular corner of Kansas knew that Mabel Wolfe thought the sun rose and set on her one and only son. Lizzie knew it didn't, of course. Never mind the obvious, the things she knew about Michael. No. Just look at the way he

19

treated his own mother and father! In all the years of Michael's supposedly meteoric rise to the top of the New York literary world, he had done absolutely nothing for the two lovely people who had brought him into the world. They still ran the paint and wallpaper supply store in Wilson Creek the same way they had for the last forty years. They still lived in the same twenties-style house; they still put slipcovers on the same sturdy furniture. By Wilson Creek standards they were well-off. By their son's standards they were just getting by. And he had done nothing for them. Nothing!

"No, I take that back," Lizzie said with a snort of disgust. "I've forgotten the color TV he gave them for Christmas a few years ago."

In a streak of unbridled generosity Michael had bought his parents a new television . . . but only after the old black-and-white had kicked off. And there were the occasional trips to New York to see him. God forbid Michael Wolfe should return to Kansas to visit his parents!

"Hey, lady, you gonna yak to yourself all afternoon or you gonna pay up?"

Lizzie blushed and smiled apologetically at her cab-driver. "How much . . . oh, here, take this and keep the change."

"Forty cents. Oh, wow. Make my day, lady."

"Did I?" She beamed. "How nice."

"Get out, will you? I got a living to make."

Lizzie stiffened. "In Kansas," she said reproachfully, stepping out of the cab, "I'm called ma'am."

"Well, thank God this ain't Kansas."

She slammed the door shut, and as the cab sped off, she realized she was standing in a puddle of some indefinable filth. New York, she thought, and laughed. She loved it! And if getting to stay here awhile required more encounters with Michael Wolfe, then so be it. No matter how handsome and successful he'd become or anything else. The man deserved to be conned—and he could afford it even more than she had anticipated. Mabel hadn't exaggerated: Michael was extremely successful.

And, if Lizzie had anyone to bet with, she'd gamble that he still couldn't beat her at King of the Hill! Even at ten, to his seventeen, she'd slaughtered him every time, and, damn it, she'd do it again!

Unless, of course, he'd been letting her win. . . .

"Ha!"

Michael Wolfe never let anyone win. It simply wasn't in the man's genes.

But, then, neither was white hair.

With an involuntary shudder Lizzie went into the hotel. She had work to do.

CHAPTER TWO

That evening Lizzie waited at her table at Il Menestrello, an elegant Italian restaurant on East Fifty-second Street and tried to look impatient, not nervous. Lizzie Olson might be shaking in her new pair of size-six high heels, but Elisabeth Guest would be calm and steady, or just plain irritated. Michael was late. Not five minutes, but fifteen—and counting. Lizzie didn't know how long she could go on nursing her one martini. She loathed martinis, but she figured that that was what a sophisticated New York designer would drink. It was what sophisticated Wichita designers drank, too, but in Wichita, Lizzie didn't give a fig about being sophisticated. In Wichita there was no Michael Wolfe to con.

She supposed she'd been lucky even to get him to agree to meet her for dinner on such short notice, but short notice—keeping him off his guard—was all part of her plan. She'd called him that afternoon after a warm, soothing bath to cure her of a case of cold feet. As expected he had been unavailable, but Gwen Duprey had promised to relay the invitation to dinner and get back to Lizzie—or Elisabeth, as she was purporting to be—right away, at which point Lizzie experienced a fluttering of the stomach and a sudden clamminess of the hands. She couldn't very well have any member of Michael Wolfe Associates calling her up at the Hotel Empire, so she gritted her teeth and insisted on an immediate answer.

To her surprise Mrs. Duprey had said, "Very well," and put Lizzie on hold. Thirty seconds later she was back with an answer: "Mr. Wolfe is anxious to have dinner with you, Ms. Guest." And so Lizzie stifled a tidal wave of panic and suggested, in the refined tones of Elisabeth Guest, that they meet at Il Menestrello at seven-thirty.

And now, as she sipped her martini, trying not to gag, Lizzie fought a relapse of her case of cold feet. Who did she think she was, going up against a man like Michael Wolfe?

"Crazy," she muttered.

Then the maitre d' was showing him to her table, and Wolfe was staring at her, looking just as magnificent and successful as he had that morning: utterly relaxed, utterly in control. Lizzie had to draw the cool, urbane look she gave him from the depths of her pioneer soul. Her ancestors had endured disease, death, droughts, fires, and war in their struggle to settle the plains. Surely she could draw on a little of their strength to handle Michael Wolfe!

"Michael?" she said with a dazzling smile. "Hello, I'm Elisabeth Guest."

He took her hand in a brief, firm grasp and sat down opposite her, still eyeing her closely. She expected an apology for being late, a demand for an explanation, *something*, but instead he asked bluntly, "What happened to your red hair?"

Her red hair? She could feel her nerve draining out of her. This wasn't supposed to be happening. Wolfe was supposed to see the dark-haired, urbane woman in black seated at the table, not the redhead in the polka-dotted bandana he'd caught standing on his desk.

She tried very hard not to pray, curse, or moan out loud, and thanked the powers that be that she had thought of Chelsea. Ad-libbing in front of Michael Wolfe was a risky business.

"Red hair? Oh, you must have met my assistant, Chelsea Barnard. She stopped by your office this morning to take some preliminary measurements for me. Won't you have a drink, Mr. Wolfe?"

He said he would and promptly ordered a martini.

Lizzie surreptitiously wiped her sweaty palms on the linen napkin on her lap, hoping he believed her explanation about the redhead he'd encountered that morning who looked like her. She covered her nervousness with a cool smile and took a sip of her martini. Not taking any chances, she'd called Chelsea that afternoon, just before calling Michael, and, after considerable cajoling, pleading, and bribing, persuaded her to fly out to New York the following day. Wolfe was going to foot the bill, but he didn't know that yet.

Chelsea had been skeptical and pointed out that she didn't have freckles, nor did she have the same hip and thigh dimensions as her "boss, the rail." Lizzie had insisted, rather shrilly, that Wolfe had been much too flabbergasted at finding a redhead on his desk to have noticed said redhead's dimensions. Red hair, however, he would notice and remember. So when Chelsea came to New York, she would have to wear a red wig.

"All right," Chelsea had said with no show of enthusiasm, "but polka-dotted bandanas are out, do you hear me? O-u-t."

"Just come, Chelsea," Lizzie had said, sounding just as relieved as she felt.

Muttering something about jail sentences, Chelsea had promised to be in New York in twenty-four hours.

Which left only tonight for Lizzie to contend with Michael Wolfe alone. She smiled at him and concentrated on being a sophisticated brunette.

His martini arrived, and he looked straight at Lizzie with eyes the same shade his hair used to be: dark, dark brown. They were intense, intelligent, and very suspicious, not the laughing eyes of the boy she had beaten at King of the Hill, nor the obnoxious, scornful eyes of the young man who had said that Wilson Creek, his hometown and hers, was hell on earth.

"Why was your assistant measuring my office?" he asked.

"Because I can't begin to redesign it until I know its dimensions," she said pleasantly. "But there's no need to worry. You just leave everything to me. You're going to have an office suite that is the envy of every literary agent in New York. You'll love it, I promise."

"You're an interior decorator," he said cagily.

"Designer," she corrected. "Of course."

Her head itched under her human-hair wig, which had cost a staggering amount of money. Back in Kansas, when she'd concocted her scheme, she'd been careful to create a successful New York interior designer who would not remind Wolfe of a redheaded teenager who'd worked at his parents store in Kansas fifteen years ago. She figured that wouldn't be hard at all, and she had figured Wolfe would be a sleazeball easily intimidated by a woman like Elisabeth Guest.

Lizzie had gone to a beauty consultant friend in Kansas City for help, and the end result was the woman sitting across from Wolfe at the small linen-covered table: a slim, elegant, ebony-haired woman wearing a dramatic black wool crepe suit by a Parisian designer, designer stockings, and high-heeled designer shoes, which were by far the most absurdly uncomfortable things she had ever put on her feet. Fortunately her friend had warned her to practice walking in them. She'd also purchased an alligator clutch purse and lapis lazuli earrings but drew the line at buying new underwear. She figured she was the only woman in the entire restaurant wearing Sears's best all-cotton briefs.

Wolfe, however, would never know that!

She smiled, hoping none of her makeup cracked. Her friend in Kansas City had shown her exactly what colors a brunette would use and how to create a look that was dramatic, confident, and totally different from what Lizzie was used to. The mess had taken almost an hour to apply—over an hour if she counted the clay mask that supposedly did good things (heaven only knew what!) to her pores.

"You look confused," she said, and opened her menu, flashing her long and one-hundred-percent-fake red nails.

Confused wasn't exactly the right word. Skeptical, suspicious, ready to pounce—those were more on target. In a thousand different ways he was not the Michael Wolfe she had expected to confront. She noticed his lashes, as thick and as dark as his eyes, a startling contrast to his white hair. Should she just whisk off her wig and admit to everything? But how could she? She'd already spent a fortune—her seed money, she called it, which she'd obtained by cashing in her last money market certificate. She was broke. Talented and honest (at least up until tonight) but impoverished. Michael would come through for her . . . she hoped.

"Come, Michael, you haven't forgotten . . . well, I suppose with your busy schedule you can't possibly remember everything, and obviously we've never met. No matter. Shall I refresh your memory?"

He leaned back and gave her a disturbing half-smile. "Please."

"All right." She cleared her throat and sat up straight. She was beginning to perspire. What would happen to her gobs of tawny makeup? To her wig? Lord, but she itched! She had hoped to intimidate Wolfe with her urbanity and sophistication. Instead she had just measured up to his . . . but only just. "We talked two months ago—"

"On the phone?"

"Yes, of course. I had been recommended to you by a mutual acquaintance."

"Who?"

Mabel Wolfe had dropped dozens of names of people her son knew, but only one of the illustrious people she had mentioned would serve Lizzie's purposes. "Isaac Pearl," she said.

Wolfe drank some of his martini and set the glass down. "He's dead."

"Yes, I know. I was at the funeral, of course."

"So was I. I didn't see you."

"Oh, you probably just didn't notice. I saw you, though. You're very distinctive, you know. In any case, I did some work for Mr. Pearl, which he was very happy with, and he mentioned me to you. And he suggested I call you myself. I'm not sure if he knew you needed a designer or if he thought you needed a designer, but, of course, things worked out." She picked up her martini glass and tried not to gulp. "Am I ringing any bells?"

"A few," he said enigmatically.

She just managed a smile. How could she be ringing any bells if the story she was telling him was a total fabrication? She hoped she wasn't ringing any wrong bells. And here she had been so sure she'd be able to read Michael's mind!

"So we talked," she went on, "and you said for me to write and give you an estimate of what it would cost to totally redecorate a six-room office suite. I balked at giving an estimate without seeing what I'd be working on, remember?"

"Frankly, no."

"Well, no matter. I came by one afternoon—you were out—and had a look around, then went back to my office and wrote you a letter. You wrote back two weeks later and accepted my offer. I then wrote to you explaining that I wouldn't be able to start work until the first of April. I never heard from you, so I assumed my schedule was agreeable to you."

The waiter appeared, and she ordered veal. Michael said he'd have his usual, which unnerved Lizzie, but only for a moment. Why shouldn't a successful literary agent know his way around an elegant New York restaurant? It was just that said successful literary agent was Michael Wolfe from Wilson Creek. That's what disconcerted her. She didn't like having to adjust her very firm preconceived notions about this man. It would have been much easier if he had simply confirmed all her prejudices.

"This has never happened before," she went on, forcing herself to continue her ruse. There just wasn't time for that now. "A client forgetting he's hired me, but it's no problem, really. I'm not offended—"

"Good," he said, his tone gruff but somehow amiable. He raised his martini glass and peered at her over its rim. She wished she hadn't noticed his eyes. If she was an editor and had to deal with Michael Wolfe on a regular basis, she would avoid direct eye contact. "And if Isaac Pearl thought you could do my offices, I guess that's good enough for me."

"Then—" Lizzie choked, speechless.

"Then it's a deal, Ms. Guest," Michael said with great aplomb but not smiling. "I won't contest."

"You mean . . . I mean . . ."

"Bring me your contract and we'll go over it point by point. You do work under contract?"

"Yes, of course. Sure. I—"

She couldn't go on. He was a pushover after all! She cleared her throat quickly and remembered that she was supposed to be a sophisticated Manhattan designer. "Excuse me for a moment, won't you?"

She rose regally from the table and made her way to the ladies' room, where she celebrated by whisking off her wig and scratching her head. Then, with a gleeful chuckle, she restored herself to being a brunette in spike heels.

Michael had ordered her and himself another martini, and now that preliminary business was concluded, he gave her a rakishly sexy smile as she returned to her seat. "You interest me, Ms. Guest," he said bluntly.

Oh, Lord, she thought, that's all I need! But now that she had him, she didn't want to lose him. "Do I? In what way?"

He laughed softly, the kind of laugh that sent shivers up and down women's spines, including Lizzie's. Just because she was from Wilson Creek and had known him at his lesser hours didn't mean she was immune to his sensual charms. Maybe, in some ways, it made her more susceptible to all that he had become. "Lots of ways," he said. "Let's just say I'm looking forward to getting to know you better."

"How nice." She already knew too much about Michael Wolfe as it was!

Their entrées arrived, and Lizzie deftly shifted the sudden personal nature of their conversation to a dis-

30

cussion of New York real estate prices. Since she'd been reading the Sunday *New York Times* for weeks, she wasn't totally out of her realm. Safe subjects flowed from there. Michael kept looking at her in strange, probing ways and smiling mysteriously. Lizzie ate as fast as she could without being rude, and refused dessert, after-dinner drinks, and going back to Michael's place for a nightcap. The very idea set her hair—both sets of it!—on end.

"I really ought to be getting back," she said firmly but not tartly. She didn't want to offend him if she could help it. "I have work to do this evening."

"So do I, as a matter of fact, but an agent's work is never done. There's always something. Allow me to drive you home, then."

"No, there's no need. Thank you."

To her relief he didn't insist but took her elbow as they left the restaurant and, outside in the cool night air, hailed her a cab. He had refused to let her pay for dinner, which was just fine with her, although she had made a show of protesting. What would he have thought if she had proceeded to pay in traveler's checks? She had to be the only thirty-one-year-old woman in the United States of America who didn't have a credit card, not one.

"I look forward to seeing you again soon, Elisabeth," he said smoothly. "It's nice to meet someone who doesn't remind me of work."

She wasn't sure just when he'd started to use her first name, but she didn't like it. "Yes," she said. What had she gotten herself into? "But you love your work just as

I love mine. That's why we're both so good at what we do, I suppose. Speaking of which, we'll need to discuss plans—your space needs and so forth."

He smiled, a touch of amusement reaching his eyes. "So we will. How about ten o'clock tomorrow morning at my office?"

"That sounds fine," she said. "Good night."

He made a move toward her, but a cab pulled alongside the curb and she leapt into it, calling out a promise to get started on his office right away. She made sure the door was closed before she told the driver to head to the Empire, and then, two blocks later, she whisked off her wig and scratched her head. Michael Wolfe was sexier than she had bargained on, much more worldly and urbane, even wealthier, but, underneath his suave good looks, he was just a pushover.

No wonder he had white hair!

For the first time Lizzie felt truly confident that her plan was going to work. Her one and only New York City contact was going to pay off! She, Lizzie Olson of Wichita, Kansas, formerly of Wilson Creek, Kansas, was going to be an interior designer in Manhattan.

And good ol' Michael was going to help her.

Later that evening Michael Wolfe made a call to Wilson Creek, Kansas. Mabel Wolfe answered the phone. They exchanged the usual pleasantries before he said, "Mother, whatever happened to Lizzie Olson?"

"Lizzie? Oh . . . um . . . well, I . . . why?"

So his mother was in on Lizzie's nutty scheme, too. That afternoon, after she'd phoned him and invited him to dinner, he had set in his office staring at his recently measured ceiling, putting pieces together: red hair; a dazzling smile; interior design; guts. She wasn't a spy; Gwen hadn't found a single thing disturbed or missing in his office. And she wasn't a New York interior designer named Elisabeth Guest because Oakes had left a memo on his desk telling him there was no New York interior designer named Elisabeth Guest and certainly not one on West Seventy-second. Oakes was nothing if not thorough. Then who the hell was this Elisabeth Guest?

And, after wracking his memory, he had come up with Lizzie Olson . . . chubby little redheaded Lizzie. She had been one of the parade of teenagers who had worked at his parents' store over the years. As he recalled she and her friend Lucy Terwilliger were two of the more memorable employees. Even then Lizzie had had a penchant for design—and meddling. She and Lucy would tell customers that their choice of bathroom wallpaper was unimaginative and recommend alternatives. But Lizzie was from a past Wolfe preferred to remember from a distance. His parents were a phone call or a plane ticket away, but he liked to think there were fifteen hundred miles and a lot of years between him and Wilson Creek. And he wanted to keep it that way. He didn't want Wilson Creek moving to New York in the form of Lizzie Olson, and it didn't matter who or what she had become.

"Michael?"

"I'm here, Mother."

Once he'd deduced that the woman standing on his

desk had to be Lizzie Olson, Wolfe had assumed his
mother was involved somehow. Where else would Lizzie
get a sheet of his stationery and Isaac Pearl's name?

"I asked you why you want to know about Lizzie,"
Mabel Wolfe said.

"Just curious," he replied.

"She's always been talented, you know."

"Yes, I know," he said dryly, thinking of her masquerade as Elisabeth Guest. "Doesn't she teach art at
the high school?"

"Oh, no, not anymore. She quit three or four years
ago. Her father died suddenly after she graduated from
college, you know, and her family desperately needed
her. Her sister Hildie was just sixteen, and Hazel had
her and the farm to manage—it was just too much. So
Lizzie got the teaching job at home and helped out for a
few years. Then Hildie married Jake Terwilliger, and
they've merged his place with the Olsons' farm, but, of
course, Hazel manages her own place. She's quite the
farmer these days. You remember Hazel, don't you?"

All too well, Wolfe thought. His own mother sounded
nervous, chattering the way she was. She knew her son
hated hearing town gossip. Talk of Wilson Creek bored
the hell out of him. "After Lizzie quit teaching where
did she move to?" he asked, steering the conversation
back on course.

"Wichita."

"To do what?"

"Work."

"Mother, are you not telling me something?"

"Don't be silly."

34

"Is Lizzie still in Wichita?"

"Well, she's talked about . . . oh, Michael, be nice to her!"

He laughed softly, thinking of the slim, stunning woman in the dark wig. "You never were a good accomplice, Mother."

"I mean it, Michael," his mother said in the same tone of voice she had used years ago to tell him to clean up his room.

"Did she ever marry?" He regretted the question immediately, but why had he asked it?"

"No," his mother replied without comment.

Wolfe was irritated with himself, but he wasn't about to take it out on his mother. "You aren't going to tell me what you two have cooked up, are you?"

He could just see his sixty-four-year-old mother pursing her lips stubbornly. He'd come by his own stubborn streak naturally. "It's not my place."

"As you wish, but don't worry about Lizzie."

"You'll be nice to her?"

"As nice as she deserves, Mother," he said, "as nice as she deserves."

After he hung up he poured himself a glass of Scotch and sat watching the Manhattan skyline, wondering what Lizzie Olson/Elisabeth Guest was up to. That they were one and the same was completely beyond doubt. It might be very interesting to play along with her little scheme. Never mind that he had refused to redecorate his offices for the past eight years and would have remembered when he'd changed his mind. Never mind that her forged letter was no more binding than a used

35

Band-Aid. Never mind that Isaac Pearl had been cremated and his memorial service had been small and private. That dazzling smile of Lizzie's had cost John Olson a couple acres worth of wheat in orthodontal fees, and Michael Wolfe remembered it.

He remembered it well.

CHAPTER THREE

At precisely ten o'clock the next morning Lizzie was standing outside Michael Wolfe's office, trying to regain last night's feeling of supreme self-confidence, even euphoria. She was going to succeed; Michael was a pushover; Michael hadn't changed that much during the past decade and a half—they were the thoughts that had lulled her to sleep. But now she remembered his penetrating gaze and mysterious smile. Who did she think she was kidding?

"Lizzie," she said to herself, "you are about to take your life into your hands."

She rubbed her hands together and turned the knob on the tacky outer door. The top half was translucent glass with gold filigreed diamonds, straight out of a hard-boiled detective novel. A smile broke out across her face as she felt her self-confidence returning. Michael Wolfe needed her help in redesigning his offices into a place befitting his stature in the literary world as much as she needed his help in establishing herself as a reputable New York interior designer!

With a burst of courage she pushed open the door. "Mrs. Duprey?" she said, smiling regally. "I'm here to see Mr. Wolfe. We have a ten-o'clock appointment."

Gwen Duprey blinked twice at the dark-haired woman in the bright-blue wool jersey dress, big silver bracelets and earrings, and black stockings and shoes. It was the sort of dress Lizzie Olson wouldn't have been caught dead wearing, but it looked rather nice on Elisabeth Guest. The problem with dressing exotically, however, was that everything she wore was so damned memorable. On the other hand no one could tell one pair of engineer pants from another. Not that Lizzie had worn engineer pants to meetings with clients back in Kansas, just nondescript clothes of good quality.

Suddenly, as if deciding whatever the woman in blue and Michael Wolfe were up to was none of her business, Gwen smiled and said pleasantly, "And you're—"

"Guest," Lizzie said. "Elisabeth Guest."

"Of course. Mr. Wolfe is on the phone, so if you'll have a seat for just a moment . . ."

Lizzie ignored the two green vinyl chairs that Gwen Duprey gestured toward in the reception area. Those chairs are beyond tacky! she thought, and she headed straight for the door to Wolfe's office, having decided an offensive move was her best defense in dealing with the man.

"No, no," Gwen protested, "you can't wait in there!"

But Lizzie was already in, pulling the door tightly shut behind her. Michael was behind his desk, a contract opened up in front of him, phone at his ear. Gwen burst in, apologizing to her employer while simultaneously wrenching Lizzie's right elbow and preparing to escort her out. Wolfe waved her off and glowered across his cluttered desk at Lizzie.

Her knees wobbled. He was in charcoal cashmere, with a plum vest and a white shirt. His hair was perfect. His eyes were clear, dark, and bold. He looked very busy and intent on whatever he was doing. *I'm in for holy hell*, Lizzie thought, but greeted him with a big, easy smile. She sat on the edge of a fake leather couch and managed not to grimace. Michael's taste in office decor was appalling. The walls were institutional green, the drapes, such as they were, were two inches too short, and she was sure the furniture had never been in style. Michael needs me, Lizzie thought, feeling better.

"Let me get back to you, Cecily," he said, hanging up.

Cecily? Lizzie wondered as she crossed her ankles, tucking them off to her left. Was Cecily an editor? A client? A woman friend? Lizzie frowned. What did it matter? Curiosity, she told herself, that's all it was.

"You look a little green at the gills, Ms. Guest," Michael said bluntly. "Something wrong?"

"Not at all. I was just thinking how different this place is going to look when I'm finished."

"You don't like it now, I take it?"

"Well . . ."

"I've been here eight years, no complaints."

"But you're a very successful literary agent."

"So?"

"So your offices should reflect your status."

"My offices should be a place to work. Period. I don't get many people up here, anyway. If I want to show off to clients or editors, I have them over to my apartment."

Lizzie wrinkled up her nose in distaste. She could just imagine what Michael Wolfe's apartment was like!

"When I'm at work," he went on, "I like to feel like I'm working."

Back in Wichita it hadn't occurred to Lizzie that Michael would be a workaholic. Somehow the fast, easy buck had seemed more his style. "I'll have to take all this into consideration, of course," she said. "I take it you prefer function and comfort over beauty?"

"Don't forget cost." He grunted. "So what do you want?"

"I need your American Express card number," she said.

"*My what*?" he asked incredulously.

She repeated her request.

He didn't answer her. He merely leaned back in his chair—more fake leather—and twisted his mouth first to one side and then to the other.

Lizzie's knees began to shake, but she told herself that that was happening because she'd only had a croissant for breakfast, In her opinion they were nothing but air. The wobbly feeling wasn't due to making an outrageous request, nor was it because she had noticed the fine, tanned muscles in Wolfe's wrist, the Cartier watch, the blunt nails, the strong, masculine hands. Simple hunger, she insisted to herself. "If you don't want to give me your American Express card number,

I'll send you a bill. Of course, I'll have to charge extra for paperwork and—"

"Tell me, Ms. Guest," he said in a voice completely different for the surly tone he'd used a moment ago, "what do people call you? Elisabeth? Beth?" He leaned forward, pausing, and folded his hands on his blotter. "I don't know, I fancy you as a Lizzie myself."

His voice was liquid, deep, sexy, *knowing*. But how could he know? He doesn't, Lizzie told herself. He couldn't possibly know. His guessing her real name was a lucky shot in the dark. She looked nothing like Lizzie Olson, not in that wig and that dress. She placed her hands on her knees—those nails were a bit much for Lizzie too—and smiled. "You do have a sense of humor, don't you, Michael? No, I'm an Elisabeth."

"Would you object if I called you Lizzie?"

"Vociferously."

Michael wasn't smiling. "Okay, *Ms. Guest*, explain why you need my American Express card number."

"Certainly." Lizzie licked her lips and launched into her prepared speech. "I sent Chelsea to Kansas City yesterday—"

"Why?"

"There was an important auction last night; a piece I had in mind for your office was up for sale. I couldn't go myself, so I sent Chelsea."

"Did she wear her polka-dotted bandana?"

Lizzie laughed to cover her growl of pure, unadulterated anger. He sounded so damned smug! Who did he think he was to judge her? A man who worked in surroundings like this had no business judging the way

41

she dressed! He could afford better. All he needed was the good taste, which he obviously didn't have.

"No, no, of course not," she said, her voice as calm and unemotional as she could make it.

"Did she get the piece?"

"No. The price went too high—far more than what it was worth—and we do like to be responsible when we spend our clients' money. We spend it just as though it were our own."

"I had that feeling, yes."

Lizzie ignored the undertone of sarcasm, refused to consider why it might be there. "Of course. That's why you hired me. My methods may be somewhat unorthodox, but they always work to my client's advantage. That's why I cut corners when I can. Which is why I need your American Express number. I have the contract, but I want to give you enough time to go over it before you sign it and give me a thirty-five percent deposit."

Wolfe looked at her warily, not amused. She tried to think about the dark-haired boy she used to push off the bales of hay they had used for a hill, the arrogant, know-it-all young man who had stormed into Wolfes' Paint and Wallpaper Supply during his breaks from college and complained about how dead Wilson Creek was, how glad he was to be out of there. How she had despised him for putting down her home—for putting down her and her family and his own parents!

And yet hadn't she dreamed of the day when she would leave Wilson Creek? Even then, at age sixteen, she couldn't imagine staying in her hometown. But,

42

after college, circumstances had forced her back for five years. She had put her plans for her future on hold; she had refused to fall for any of the men she had grown up with; she had plotted and prayed for the day when she would be able to leave. Who was she now to criticize Michael for wanting out—for getting out? She was no better than he was!

"Lizzie?"

His voice was soft, concerned, filled with sensitivity, with the sounds of the years gone by, lived well, happily. He was thirty-eight and had done so much. She was thirty-one and had done so little. And there was nothing she could do to change that, nothing.

"Please excuse me," she said, suddenly leaping to her feet. Fighting unwelcome tears, she ran out of Wolfe's office.

Wolfe wondered what he'd said, but intuitively he knew he hadn't said or done anything wrong. Lizzie was her own worst problem. Pretty, dazzling Lizzie. Sneaky Lizzie. Troubled Lizzie. Tears in her wide blue eyes, panic in her face—and he'd just let her go. He could have intercepted her at the door, at the elevator, said something. But he hadn't. And now she was off alone, upset.

It serves her right, he thought. *Trying to get my American Express number!*

He slammed his fist down on the slate blotter, picked up the phone, and impulsively called his mother. "Does Chelsea Barnard exist?" he demanded.

"Michael? Is that you?"

"Of course."

"Yes, well. Chelsea, you say? She's Lizzie's . . . assistant."

"You hesitated."

"I was turning down the coffee."

"Can't I get a straight answer out of anyone?"

"Michael, calm down. You'll get ulcers."

"I already have ulcers. Mother, is Lizzie Olson a designer?"

"Of course. One of the best. She's won awards."

"Then why in the name of hell didn't she come to me as herself and ask me as a friend—"

"I don't think she considers you a friend, but it's more complicated than that."

"I'm listening."

"She lost money, Michael."

"So? We all lose money once in a while. If she's good, she'll bounce back."

"No, no, you don't understand. She . . . oh, never mind. I really shouldn't say."

"She went bankrupt? What?"

"I'm not going to tell you. If she wants you to know, she can tell you herself. Just remember, she's a fighter and a cheerful soul. Nothing gets her down."

"But the bottom line is that she has no money, right?"

"She made a mistake that with your help she's going to overcome."

"What about this Chelsea?"

"Chelsea has stood by Lizzie for a long time, Michael."

"Then she's in New York?"

"Not that I know of. There just wasn't enough money—"

44

Hence Lizzie's request for his American Express card number. Now he understood. "Thanks, Mother."

He went out to the front office, sent Gwen on a made-up errand, and sat at her typewriter. He rolled a sheet of his stationery in, typed the date—

And then stopped.

He didn't have Lizzie's real address—God only knew where she was staying—and he couldn't very well address the letter to the fake West Seventy-second Street address. And if he wrote out a check to tide her over until they worked out the contract, which he fully intended to do, God help him, how was Lizzie going to cash the check if it had Elisabeth Guest's name on it?

"Hell."

Why should he want to help that conniving, crooked woman, anyway? What he ought to do was pay her way back to Kansas, refuse to pay Chelsea's way to New York, and offer to lend her enough money to get back on her feet in Wichita. God forbid that he set her up for a career in New York! One former resident of Wilson Creek exiled to Manhattan was enough. Wolfe had never known himself to be irrationally generous, and he was damned if he was going to start now. Damned, too, if he was going to help some down-on-her-luck, scheming woman from Wilson Creek!

Too bad she didn't look anything like what he had always imagined a grown-up Lizzie Olson would look like. And act like.

Damn it, he thought, *why the hell am I so intrigued by her?*

He couldn't afford to be intrigued. Or nice.

So why was he going to let her redesign his offices?

He wondered what exactly Lizzie wanted from him. Money, so she could resume her career in Wichita? Or a start on a career in New York?

He ripped the sheet of paper out of the typewriter and crumpled it up with a vengeance. When Meg Oakes came in to ask him a question about one of her clients' royalty statements, he said, "Oakes, tell that husband of yours I know how he felt when you were playing two people."

Meg frowned, confused. "Wolfe, what are you talking about?"

"Just tell him," Wolfe said, and he stalked back into his office.

Lizzie stopped at a coffee shop and ordered scrambled eggs, three strips of bacon, two pieces of toast and jelly, and black coffee. After she ate she felt much better. As she nursed a second cup of coffee she debated how she was going to make up for her latest blunder. Running out of Wolfe's office with tears in her eyes like some silly twerp! What a mess of things she was making. She had to get that money off Michael. There was no way she could pay for Chelsea's plane ticket if she expected to pay her hotel bill and eat three meals a day this week. Chelsea had said she could swing her own meals, and Lizzie had volunteered to let her bunk in the second twin bed in her room at the Empire. It would be cramped, but they'd endured worse together over the years.

First, though, Lizzie had to get Chelsea to New York.

She downed the last of her coffee and faced the brutal reality of her situation: She had to go to Michael with her tail between her legs. While apologizing she would somehow inform him in no uncertain terms that he was not to call her Lizzie. Their relationship was and would remain strictly professional.

But what if he already knew who she was?

She shuddered and shook her head. No, that was impossible. She looked nothing like, acted nothing like, *was* nothing like that chubby, carefree teenager Michael had known years ago in Kansas. There was nothing left of that girl but those hidden wisps of red hair.

Lizzie could have gotten Chelsea halfway to New York on what she paid for her breakfast, but she supposed the expense was well worth the results: her knees had stopped wobbling. She fixed her wig and headed back down to Michael Wolfe's office.

He was flagging a cab outside his building when Lizzie approached him. "Michael, I'm so glad I caught you," she said breezily. "Pleae forgive me for running out like that. I must be allergic to something in your office."

Michael frowned at her. "Could it be my fake leather furniture?" he asked mockingly.

She laughed lightly, the way she imagined a sophisticated New Yorker would. "That's very funny, Michael." A cab screeched to a halt in front of Michael. Without a word he clamped a hand on her arm, tore open the cab's rear passenger door, and shoved her in before him.

"Michael!" she protested, shocked and indignant.

He gave the driver his destination—Fifth Avenue and Fifty-fifth Street—and held on tightly to Lizzie. Then, somehow, his arm settled around her shoulders. Lizzie's wig had slipped, but no red hairs were poking out, or at least she hoped not. But this was only a passing thought, a fleeting worry. Her thoughts were focused on the feel of Michael's arm around her. Her entire body was focused on the feel of Michael's arm around her. His touch was strong, secure, and maddeningly sensual.

Wolfe was surprised at his own reaction. He had snatched Lizzie with the same neutral vigor with which he had pushed her around in their childhood games twenty years ago. He hadn't thought of her as a woman then, and so he didn't expect to think seriously of her as a woman now, despite the mounting evidence to the contrary. Last night they had both been playacting, but now he wasn't. He didn't know about Lizzie. Maybe she was, maybe she wasn't. It didn't matter. The blue eyes he was looking into were those of a woman. The firm yet delicate shoulder on which his hand rested was definitely that of a woman, a woman of strength and spirit, not just any woman. Lizzie Olson. Beneath that ridiculous wig were Lizzie's thick red locks. Beneath that carefully applied tawny makeup were Lizzie's golden freckles and milky-white skin. Try as she would, there was nothing she could do to change the facts: She was Lizzie Olson, and Wolfe knew it . . . and approved. *God help me*, he thought, *but I do*. Without being aware of it he began caressing her shoulder with his hand.

Lizzie pulled away from him, edging toward the opposite end of the seat. "What do you think you're doing?"

Wolfe grinned. "Spiriting you away. I'm on the run all day today, but I want to talk to you."

She looked at him warily but his grin faded, and he adopted a more serious, businesslike demeanor. *If he can*, she thought, *I can*. And she did. "What do you wish to talk about?" she asked in her deep Elisabeth Guest voice.

"First, I wouldn't want to increase your paperwork or my bill, so give the information on this Chelsea Barnard's flight to Gwen and we'll take care of it."

"That sounds fine. It was only that I trusted you to keep your word in the letter, Michael, and so I agreed to send Chelsea to Kansas City on your behalf. You and I know we have a binding agreement—"

"Spare me. Do you have a contract for me?"

"Not on me, no, but I have one prepared."

"Then you can bring it to my place tonight. Central Park South, the Xavier Building. Gwen can give you directions—"

"I know the building." She didn't, really.

"Fine. I'll expect you at seven. I'm having a few people over for cocktails. You'll want to get a 'feel' for my life-style before you redesign my office, won't you?"

You are not Lizzie Olson, she told herself, *therefore you will not make any sarcastic remarks*. But she couldn't wait to see just how tasteless Wolfe's apartment was. "Of course," she said airily.

He gave her a sideways look. "I suppose you'll charge me?"

49

"Anything that isn't specified in the contract will cost you seventy dollars an hour," she replied without hesitation.

"Seventy! For me to give you drinks?"

"If it's part of the interview process, which you're already being charged for, or simply to sign the contract, then no."

"It's a damned party!"

She sniffed. "I don't go to clients' parties, Mr. Wolfe, without good reason. It'll take you five minutes to sign the contract and then—"

"Ha, you don't know me, Ms. Guest. I negotiate contracts every day, and I didn't get enough money to pay an expensive New York decorator by signing them in five minutes. And a thirty-five-percent deposit is going to cost me twenty thousand dollars. I want to be damned sure about what I'm signing."

"I'll use the money wisely, Michael," Lizzie assured him.

"You damned well better. How much of the total fee is yours?"

"Most will go toward paying for furniture, carpeting, painters, carpenters, and so forth, but a small percentage will, of course, reimburse me for my time."

Wolfe was unimpressed. "How much?"

"Ten thousand, minimum. That entails certain specified tasks. Anything above and beyond is charged to you on an hourly basis."

"Seventy dollars an hour," Wolfe grumbled.

Lizzie smiled coolly. "It could be more. My rates are very reasonable, you know."

"You'd better be damned good at what you do."

He expected, perhaps even half hoped, that she would crumple and beg him to help her get back to Kansas. But she simply looked at him with that cool, level smile and said, "I am."

"I love a confident woman," Wolfe said irritably but truthfully.

The cab pulled to the curb on the corner of Fifth and Fifty-fifth, and Wolfe paid the driver and started out. Lizzie sat primly against the other door. He fought a mad urge to kiss her on her smirking red lips. Damn, how could Lizzie Olson of all people do this to him! Not clean him out of thousands of dollars—that was just a detail—but to stir him up like this? She just marched into his life and started messing things up.

"Seven o'clock," he snapped.

"Fine, I'll be there."

"By the way, who should I make the check payable to?"

"Manhattan Designs, Inc.," Lizzie replied, glad she was prepared for this one. She'd changed the name of her original company, Olson Designs. "Michael, don't look so suspicious. The designer-client relationship should be grounded in trust."

"Guess I've seen too many relationships grounded in trust go sour, Ms. Guest," he said as his parting shot.

Feeling guilty, Lizzie watched him hop out of the cab. Even on Fifth Avenue he looked suave, in control. She supposed she was glad that Michael had become such a success, and, if she went through with her plans to redesign his offices, his prestige would work to her

51

advantage, at least more than if he'd been the manipulative agent in maroon polyester that she'd imagined. But if only he were just a little less incorruptible! Then she might not feel quite so awful.

She told the driver to return to Wolfe's offices and sat back, sighing miserably. Could she continue to violate Michael's trust? Why not tell him everything now and hope for the best?

"Because he'd turn me out on my ear, that's why," she said aloud.

She'd gone too far, expended too much energy and hope, to turn back now. And she wasn't *really* violating his trust. She'd only lied about a few things: her name; Chelsea; Isaac Pearl; being a New York designer. The essentials were not lies; she was a good interior designer, and she did charge seventy dollars an hour. Well, sixty-five in Wichita.

"You're a dishonest snake in the grass, Lizzie Olson," she said to herself.

There was only one thing to do. She would design Michael a smashing, perfectly fantastic office suite . . . and, in the meantime, hope he didn't blow her and her scheme out of the water. She had the feeling that the man could be quite merciless when he so chose.

This was confirmed not twenty minutes later when Lizzie was asking Gwen Duprey how to get to Michael's place on Central Park South. With great efficiency and no questions Gwen had already contacted Chelsea and the airline and arranged for her flight to New York that evening.

"He lives in the Winthrop Building," Gwen explained. "It's a few blocks down from—"

"The Winthrop? But I thought he said Xavier."

"There's no Xavier on Central Park South, Ms. Guest."

"There isn't?" Lizzie said, sagging and lapsing into her Kansas twang. Catching herself, she snapped up straight and deepened her voice. "My mistake."

Memorizing Gwen's directions, she headed back to the hotel to become Lizzie Olson for a few hours and mull over how she was going to get out of this one.

CHAPTER FOUR

That evening, while Lizzie was dressing for Michael's cocktail party, Chelsea Barnard arrived. They embraced, patted each other on the back, and laughed. And then Chelsea closed the door to Lizzie's unprepossessing hotel room and gave her friend a grave look. "Lizzie," she said as she turned the dead-bolt lock, "there is no way on God's green earth," she went on as she slipped the chain lock into place, "that we are going to live through this." She crossed her arms over her blue-and-white-striped rugby shirt and leaned against the door. "We're dead, Lizzie."

Chelsea was creative, energetic, and flaky. She also had a tendency to exaggerate, which Lizzie knew and understood. For the first twelve years of her life Chelsea had never stepped foot out of Wilson Creek, Kansas—and then it was to visit her dying grandmother in a Wichita hospital. Chelsea's parents were hardworking and honest people, but they had health problems, bad luck, and no financial resources. Life wasn't easy. But

Wichita had changed Chelsea's life. "It's a big world out there," she'd said upon returning home, "and one of these days I'm going to see all of it."

"I know things might seem a little bleak at times," Lizzie said, "but we've survived worse."

Chelsea flopped onto the second twin bed. "I'm not so sure."

But they had, and they both knew it. In high school they'd worked desperately hard for good grades. After school and during the summer they'd worked at Wolfe's Paint and Wallpaper Supply and stashed their pay. It was for the future, for college, for a life beyond Wilson Creek. They weren't waiting for knights on white horses. They were just looking for the right horses to jump on and fly. Chelsea hadn't been Chelsea then, but Lucille Terwilliger, blond, buxom, sassy Lucy. After high school, while Lizzie went off to college, Lucy pooled all her resources and bought a one-way ticket to London. She changed her name to Chelsea Barnard after hearing the English pronounce Lucille Terwilliger. "They made it sound as though I ought to be selling stocks and bonds," she'd written to Lizzie.

Lizzie never knew exactly what had happened to Chelsea during her years in London. A year ago she had come back to Kansas, knocked on Lizzie's door, and said she needed a job. Lizzie gave her one, no questions asked. It turned out that Chelsea had become a free spirit and, somehow simultaneously, an incredibly talented, if impoverished artist. She claimed she could do anything from wallpaper around toilets to copy a Rembrandt painting, and she could.

Until disaster struck they'd made a great team.

"I've seen his picture, Lizzie," Chelsea said, breaking the heavy silence.

"Michael's?"

"No, Abraham Lincoln's. Of course Michael's! I drove out to Wilson Creek last night and had a chat with Ma Wolfe, and she showed me a picture of Michael with Ross Greening. You've seen it, haven't you?"

Lizzie faltered. "Well . . ."

"No, Lizzie! Don't tell me you haven't seen it. The one taken at the Four Seasons with Michael wearing a tuxedo and that I'm-going-to-swallow-you-alive grin? Oh, Lizzie. Lizzie, Lizzie. You had no idea what you were getting yourself into, did you?" Chelsea groaned and kicked off her sneakers. "Maybe if I go to sleep now, I'll wake up and find myself on a remote island in the Pacific surrounded by hungry cannibals. It would be better than this."

"You can't do that," Lizzie said calmly, sitting on her bed and regluing one of her fingernails. "We have to be at Michael's at seven. I think he'll want to meet you. You did bring the wig, didn't you?"

"I'm going to look like Little Orphan Annie, Liz."

"Michael won't care—so long as you have red hair. Move it, Chels. If we pull this one off, he's going to hand us a check for twenty thousand dollars."

"Twenty thous—" Chelsea hopped up. "I'll be ready in ten minutes."

Lizzie blew lightly on her fingernail. "You've only got five."

She took fifteen, but the time was well spent. Chelsea had a little more hip and bust, and her face didn't resemble Lizzie's at all, but her wig was a gorgeous shade of red, if not a little too curly. Not a single one of Chelsea's long blond tendrils showed. And Chelsea had made a seemingly smooth transition from the paint-bespeckled pants Lizzie had worn to measure Michael Wolfe's ceiling (but which Chelsea never would have worn) to a loose-fitting silk dress with a bold raspberry-and-blue pattern.

Lizzie was fooled. Now, she hoped, if only Michael would be, too.

Michael wasn't fooled—he wasn't even amused—when the two women joined his cocktail party. Two dozen people had already gathered in the spacious, modern living room of his impressive apartment overlooking Central Park. They were mostly publishing people—editors, agents, writers, a few vice-presidents—but, for variety, he had invited a few people outside the industry, too, the two women of Manhattan Interiors, Inc., among them. Wolfe talked himself out of whisking off their wigs and demanding to know what in hell was going on, but even he had to admit that they were a fetching pair. Elisabeth Guest, a.k.a. Lizzie Olson, of Wilson Creek, Kansas, was wearing an understated dress of deep plum wool, delicate black shoes, and spice-colored cosmetics. The woman next to her had to be the infamous Chelsea Barnard. Even with the outrageous red wig she looked vaguely familiar. Or was he getting paranoid? No matter. Whoever she was, she was not the woman he'd found standing on his desk yesterday morning. Too much bust, too much hip, no freckles. But, of course, he had known she wouldn't be.

They were a hopeless cause, he thought, and if he had any sense, he'd send them back to Kansas. He was getting impatient with the games, and the stunning smile Lizzie was giving him as she caught his eye across the room didn't help. He wanted to sweep her into his arms and kiss her until her wig fell off and her fake fingernails came unglued. Maybe he would—later.

"Hell, what are you thinking?" he grumbled, appalled at himself.

But as he watched Lizzie stride through the crowd he kept imagining the softness of her mouth on his. She grabbed a martini off a tray and took a practiced sip, her smile never wavering. Wolfe stiffened, steeling himself against her charms. Lizzie Olson was a hometown girl. He couldn't hurt her, but he couldn't become involved with her, either. Just being from Wilson Creek meant she knew things about him that no one else knew, some of them things he himself wanted to forget. And that was exactly how he wanted to keep it. His life was ten steps removed from Kansas, and it would stay that way. He did *not* need this nutty, beguiling redhead to blunder into his life and turn it upside down.

Then why was he about to give her a check for twenty thousand dollars and turn her loose on his office?

"Michael, how are you?" she said, proferring one gorgeously manicured hand. The hands holding the yardstick to his ceiling yesterday morning had been just as gorgeous, but the nails had been short and manageable. Wolfe noticed details. Lizzie quickly pulled her hand from his, leaving him to wonder if the physical contact distracted her too. "I'm glad I decided to come after all," she went on, her voice giving no hints. "Seeing where you live will help me redesign your office. I must say, though, this was unexpected."

Wolfe smiled enigmatically. "And what did you expect? More fake leather?"

"Something like that," she admitted with a laugh.

"I suppose I don't blame you. I moved here about a year ago and had Lorraine Kunin design the interior. I'll let her know you approve."

Wolfe took a perverse pleasure in watching Lizzie choke on her martini. But he took a greater, and not at all perverse, pleasure in rubbing the curve of her shoulder to make sure she wouldn't collapse on his carpet, not that it wouldn't have served her right. Lorraine Kunin was one of the top interior designers in New York—and one of the most expensive. He knew it, and so, obviously, did Lizzie.

"Are you all right?" he asked, properly solicitous.

"Yes, fine—a little too eager with my drink. It's been a long day." Interminable, she added to herself, but she stood up straight, recovering. "Yes, I thought this was Lorraine's work."

She had too. When they'd entered the lavish apartment, Lizzie had muttered to Chelsea, "This can't be Wolfe's place. He must have rented it." And Chelsea had muttered back, "Looks like Kunin's work to you?" To which Lizzie had replied, "Oh, lordy, it sure does." It was at that point that she'd caught Michael's eye and given him her stunning smile. The only silver lining in this black, black cloud was that if Michael could afford Lorraine Kunin, he could afford Elisabeth Guest.

"I had planned to ask her to do my office this winter," Wolfe was saying with a smug, secretive smile. "But if you come with Isaac Pearl's stamp of approval . . . well, he was a demanding man."

"True," Lizzie said blithely, "and, of course, Lorraine's strength is residential interiors. I think you'll be happier with my work."

This time it was Wolfe who choked on his martini. The gall of the woman! But he supposed anyone willing to con him had to have an impregnable ego. He liked women who thought well of themselves. Simpering martyrs did nothing for him at all.

"Oh, and Michael," she went on, "you did want me to come tonight, didn't you?"

"Yes, of course."

"I wasn't sure when you gave me the wrong address. The Xavier is on Park Avenue." That little tidbit had come from a cabdriver who had irately explained that a quarter was an insult, not a tip. Lizzie had apologized, tipped him fifteen percent, and asked about the Xavier. She smiled at Wolfe and took another sip of the awful martini. "I wasn't paying attention when you said it was on Central Park South. Was that a joke—or were you testing me for some mysterious reason?"

Furrowing his dark brows, Wolfe touched his crystal glass to hers. "*Touché*, Lizzie," he said quietly.

"Elisabeth," she corrected, "and I don't know what you're talking about."

"Trust."

Lizzie wanted to slither out of the room on her belly, but instead she looked straight at him; rather courageously, she thought. "I still don't know what you're talking about."

"Later," he said, moving close.

Very naturally, without any self-consciousness, he placed his palm on her back, just below the collar of her dress. He touched her hair, surprised at how real it felt, how soft, but he wanted to touch the thick, red locks he'd seen poking out of that bright blue bandana. Then he saw the color rising in her cheeks, the incipient panic in her wide blue eyes, and he snatched his hand away. What the hell was he doing? Scaring her, scaring himself. Damn it, though, he wasn't sorry!

"Look," he said gruffly, angry with himself, "why don't you introduce me to your assistant."

"Sure," Lizzie mumbled, looking away from Michael's dark eyes, where there was softness and depth, not gruffness. She flagged down Chelsea, who had already inserted herself into a loud, happy group. But she excused herself and joined Lizzie. "Michael, I'd like you to meet my assistant, Chelsea Barnard. Chelsea, Michael Wolfe—no, wait, you two have already met, haven't you?"

"Not formally," Chelsea said. "Mr. Wolfe, it's good to see you again. Sorry about rushing out yesterday morning, but you know how it is."

"More ceilings to measure?" Wolfe tipped his glass back and drained the last of his martini. Then he casually held the glass in two fingers and gave the two women a half-smile. "I could have sworn you had freckles, Ms. Barnard."

"Really?" She laughed. "Must be the red hair. People always assume redheads have freckles. And, please, call me Chelsea."

They weren't that good, Wolfe thought. If he'd wanted to, he could have sliced them to ribbons right there on the spot. Chelsea's feet were at least two sizes bigger than Lizzie's. Chelsea's face, attractive though it was, was completely different: more angular, a longer nose, a straighter mouth. And more than vaguely familiar. He'd seen this woman before, somewhere. But a name like Chelsea Barnard he'd have remembered—unless, of course, it was just as fake as her red hair and her boss's name.

"Did you say something?" Lizzie asked.

He'd muttered some unrepeatable oath. "No," he lied smoothly. "Why don't I introduce you to some people?"

"You go ahead, Elisabeth," Chelsea said. "I need to visit the powder room."

As Chelsea breezed off Lizzie marveled at her assistant's performance. Michael hadn't even fazed her! And if Chelsea's knees were balking at supporting her, as Lizzie's were, it didn't show. But perhaps Michael didn't have the same effect on Chelsea. To Lizzie he smelled of expensive cologne, cashmere, and success, and the effect was as intoxicating as the martini she was forcing herself to drink.

He slipped his arm around her shoulders, and she went with him and tried to be regal and disciplined and distant but failed. She wanted to sit down with him somewhere quiet and talk about what was happening, tell him who she was, ask him about the past fifteen, twenty years. What had he been doing, thinking, feeling? How did his past fit into who he was now? Who was the man who lived in this fantastically beautiful apartment, the man who worked in that awfully ugly office? She wanted to get to know him, she wanted to be friends, which, she knew, was only asking for trouble. That wasn't part of her plan.

Finally he left her with Meg Oakes and her husband, Jonathan McGavock, who was, Lizzie thought, one of the most intriguing men she'd ever met, not to mention handsome. They both called Michael by his last name, and Jonathan referred to him twice as "that scoundrel." But, clearly, they both liked him.

"He is a good agent, isn't he?" Lizzie asked.

"I'd fire him if he wasn't," Jonathan said. "He knows what he wants and he goes after it until he gets it."

"But he's scrupulous?"

"A top-notch agent has to be," Meg explained. "And I wouldn't stay with him if he wasn't, but he hates to be crossed."

"That my love, is an understatement," Jonathan said dryly.

Lizzie wondered if conning Michael, as she was, could be considered crossing him.

"Elisabeth?" Meg asked, concerned. "Are you all right? You look a little pale."

"Just tired," she said, and managed a smile.

Jonathan peered at her. "I think you'd better talk to her, Meg."

Without explaining further he walked away. Meg sighed. "I think I know what Wolfe meant this afternoon," she said, more to herself than to Lizzie. "I have a feeling, Elisabeth, that you're not everything you're claiming to be, and, believe me, I know how you feel. If you want to talk, give me a call, okay?"

"But I'm not—"

"Please. When you're ready, we can talk. Jonathan isn't a man to cross, either, but I did cross him, and, as you can see, things worked out." She smiled broadly. "One way to keep yourself from being burned at the stake is to marry the man you've crossed!"

For the second time that night Lizzie choked on her martini.

Lizzie did what she could to blend into the crowd, to drink and be merry, to imagine Michael's sad-looking office and forget this magnificent apartment, and to ignore the stirring inside her that was unprofessional and disturbing. She looked out the window and saw not the lights of Manhattan but the reflection of Michael behind her. Laughing, his dark eyes dancing, he mingled with clients, guests, and friends. Lizzie admired his polish. It wasn't an affectation but an integral part of the person Michael Wolfe had become. Perhaps it had been a part of him all along that she'd never noticed.

Alongside his social graces she sensed an underlying ruthlessness. It was there in his asides to Cecily, who turned out to be a tall, chain-smoking, straight-talking editor. It was there in the way he introduced shy new clients to old clients and urged them toward editors. It was there even in the occasional sideways glances he offered Lizzie. The polish was a part of his charm—and his ruthlessness: Michael Wolfe simply was a man who didn't like to be crossed.

But I used to beat him at King of the Hill, Lizzie reminded herself.

Then she noticed his lean waist, the way his pants, shirt, and belt all met neatly, loosely, not vying with even the slightest bulge. She would hate to try to knock him off any hill he'd conquered.

But I graduated with high honors and he barely made honors, she remembered. And then she looked around at the famous writers who were his clients and relied on his advice, the interesting, intelligent people who were his friends. Lizzie was confident in her own abilities and proud of who she was and where she came from. But she was no dummy. With just a few words Michael Wolfe could ruin her. She knew that as well as she knew anything.

Clearly she had picked the wrong man to con.

She gulped the last of her martini and plopped down on the cream-colored couch. She knew its designer, construction, and price, and shuddered at all three. *I'm doomed*, she thought. There was nothing to do but come clean, admit everything, and hope for the best.

"Don't look so glum, Lizzie," Chelsea admonished as she breezed over to her friend.

"Don't let Michael hear you call me Lizzie," Lizzie hissed. "It's Elisabeth!"

"Oh, yeah, I forgot." Chelsea grinned, unruffled. "Don't fret. He's over on the other side of the room eating some editor alive."

"That's just an hors d'oeuvre. I think I'm the main course."

"My, my," Chelsea said, "but what happened to all your spunk? As I recall, you were the one who was going to eat *Michael* alive. Losing your nerve?"

Lizzie scowled. "Wouldn't you?"

"If I were to judge him strictly on outward appearances, you're darned right I would. A couple of hours ago I'd have helped you pack your bags, but now I don't know. I like Meg, and I like Jonathan. If Michael was a total cretin, would they stay with him?"

"He's good at what he does. I've never denied that. But let's put this another way. If he's not a 'total cretin,' do I have any business conning him?"

"You can't have it both ways, *Elisabeth*. And guilt won't pay the bills. Remember, you're a damned good designer. Look, Jonathan and Meg have invited me to dinner. I thought I'd go along and see what I could learn about our friend Michael. I can talk space needs with Meg, too, if you want."

Lizzie shook her head dispiritedly. "I don't think that'll be necessary."

"How come? I think she should have some say in how you redo her office. Oh, Lord. You're not thinking of confessing, are you?"

"Just enjoy yourself, Chels. Don't worry about work."

"Don't do anything rash, okay?"

"Don't worry. Do you need some cash?"

"Why, do you have any?"

"Just traveler's checks."

"Forget it. I'll let them pay. I barely have enough for the subway. See you later, Liz."

With a parting scowl Lizzie watched Chelsea flit through the crowd toward her two new friends. How could she be so cheerful! Lizzie grabbed the last martini off a tray and took a healthy swallow. She was developing a taste for the ghastly things.

The guests began saying their good nights, and, almost all at once, the big, open apartment was quiet. Lizzie stared at her drink and wondered who had started putting olives in martinis, and what she was going to tell Mabel Wolfe, and how she was going to pay for her and Chelsea's tickets back to Kansas. She couldn't just click her heels together and say "There's no place like home."

Oh, hell, she thought, what did Dorothy know, anyway?

"Well, don't we look miserable," Michael said cheerfully, sitting down beside her.

His nearness, his smile, his dark eyes—everything about him made Lizzie want to sit back and laugh and enjoy herself. Just be with him. But she couldn't shake that nasty feeling of doom. "Michael," she said gravely, "I have a confession to make."

He looked at her knowingly and said softly, "I know you do."

"You do?"

"Mmm."

He was sitting sideways, facing her, with one arm stretched across the back of the couch. For the life of him he didn't understand why he was going to say what he was about to say. He'd faced gloomier women before; he'd listened to worse confessions than hers. And Lizzie deserved to suffer for what she was doing to him, dammit!

No, not suffer, he thought, irritated with himself for being so absurdly empathetic. But it was true. Lizzie was filled with energy, good cheer, and life—as well as a few lies—and he didn't want to be the one to shatter her dreams.

"You impersonated your assistant yesterday morning," he said abruptly. "The great Elisabeth Guest doesn't do site measurements, and Chelsea was already on her way to Kansas City. So you put on a red wig and pretended to be her. You didn't expect to run into me, and I doubt you expected me to have such a good eye."

He could see the relief washing through her, the energy and spunk returning. The sad look of gloom that had clouded her face vanished: she was ready to lie again. "You mean—" she began, stopped as she felt a pang of guilt, and then went on, exultant, "You mean you knew all along?"

"I guess, but I didn't know for sure until I met Chelsea."

"And you don't mind?"

He edged closer, finding it impossible to stay away from her. She smelled of a light, airy perfume. "You did say you were a little unorthodox," he suggested.

"That's true. Lorraine Kunin would never have done such a thing."

Wolfe had to laugh at the thought: Lorraine Kunin

was *not* unorthodox. "No, I suppose not. Tell me, were the engineer pants yours?"

"Yes—left over from college."

Ah, she thought, it felt so good to lie again, and without a qualm! She decided Michael was wonderful, and if he'd been any less physically appealing, she'd have kissed him.

"I was afraid they wouldn't fit," she added with a sly smile.

"Oh, they did. I noticed."

"Yes, well . . ." She cleared her throat, chastising herself for having, in her relief, sounded so friendly and approachable—that wasn't how Elisabeth Guest would behave, that was Lizzie Olson. "Well, I'm glad you understand, and I'm glad I told you. Do you suppose we could keep this our secret?"

Wolfe was imaging all sorts of delicious ways he could blackmail her. "Of course."

Lizzie's brows were knit in concentration. "You'll want concessions in the contract, won't you?"

Wolfe coughed, covering his surprised laugh. No wonder Lizzie had gone broke! Before sending her back to Kansas, he'd have to give her a few lessons in contract negotiations. "Why don't I look at the contract first?" he suggested gravely.

"Sure."

Lizzie bounced up and went for her pocketbook. Wolfe leaned sideways against the couch and never took his eyes off her slender frame. Even her ankles drove him to distraction! He liked her easy movements, her strength, her agility. He tried to concentrate on the amount of money he was about to sign away to her but to no avail. He kept imagining how Lizzie's arms would feel around him, her mouth on his, her legs intertwined with his. Having her stay after the cocktail party had been a mistake because now he didn't want her to leave.

She handed him the contract and purposely sat on the chair kitty-corner to the couch. Wolfe smiled to himself: so he wasn't the only one feeling the sparks flashing between them. His whole damned body was tingling with a desire he hadn't felt in years. God help them both, but he was glad.

"It's self-explanatory," she said.

"I think I can manage."

To his surprise she laughed merrily, the kind of unselfconscious laughter that reminded him of good friends and all the possibilities of love and romance. "Yes, I suppose you can," she agreed. "I keep forgetting you're an agent."

"Now that's a first," he said pleasantly. "What else would I be?"

His eyes widened, just for a second, and her laugh faltered, but she recovered quickly—expertly—and said congenially, with a smile, "A client who *desperately* needs his office overhauled."

The contract looked fair, protecting her interests and, to a lesser extent, his. He blinked twice at the sum Lizzie's interior designs would cost him. But when he looked over at her sitting on the edge of her chair, wearing that ridiculous wig yet looking so hopeful and beautiful, a sharp pang of desire mixed with affection for her made him grudgingly admit that it was high time he parted with some money to spruce up his office. Besides, he rationalized, Lorraine Kunin would charge him almost twice as much without providing half as much fun.

When he'd finished reading, he withdrew a pen from an inner pocket and did something he *never* did: he signed the contract without changing a single word. Lizzie watched, clutching her knees. Then he pulled the check from his billfold and handed it and the contract over to her.

"Dinner?" he said.

She shook her head.

"I've got avocado and blue cheese salad, good wine, bread—just a light supper, really."

"No, I couldn't possibly think of dinner after eating so many hors d'oeuvres."

She hadn't touched a single one, and Wolfe knew it. The woman couldn't eat because he'd just given her twenty thousand dollars and the surprise of her life! *She probably thinks I'm a sap*, he thought. But he knew the truth: he'd signed a legal, binding contract, and if Lizzie Olson/Elisabeth Guest didn't live up to her end of the deal, he'd sue the pants off her.

"Michael, are you all right?"

"Fine," he said curtly.

"I think I had one martini too many. I'm going to head home." She rose unsteadily, her right hand clenching the contract and check. "Thank you for a lovely evening—for everything. It's going to be a pleasure working with you, Michael."

Half reluctantly, half stoically, Wolfe got her coat and

71

helped her with it. Lizzie, however, teetered, and he politely caught her.

Before either knew what was happening, knew who had set what in motion, their mouths met and their bodies were pressed together. Lizzie sighed, deeply satisfied by the warmth of his arms and the delicious sensations his kisses were sparking in her. She felt the hunger in him and in herself, and kissed him back eagerly, knowing exactly what she was doing and not wanting to stop. His hands slipped inside her coat and grasped her buttocks firmly, pulling her intimately against him as his tongue trailed across her lips and into her mouth.

The unmistakable ache of desire spread through her, and she wrapped her arms tightly around him, feeling the fine, hard muscles of his back, letting her hands wander through his thick, white hair. She couldn't believe she, Lizzie Olson, was here in New York kissing Michael Wolfe, her childhood enemy. Really, she was aching for more than just his kisses.

But then he touched her hair, and she quickly pulled away from him, remembering the wig, the makeup, the fake fingernails she was wearing. Michael wasn't kissing her. He was kissing Elisabeth Guest. That's who he wanted, not Lizzie Olson.

Mumbling good night, she fled out the door.

For five solid minutes after she left Wolfe cursed himself and her. He kicked a chair. He gathered up stray glasses and dumped them in the sink, breaking one. What in the hell was the matter with the woman? One minute she was responding so eagerly, so wildly to him, and the next she was fleeing like a scared chipmunk.

He cursed some more.

More to the point, *What in hell has gotten into me?*

He had vowed he wouldn't touch her. He had vowed to be chaste and paternalistic toward her, to help her along and get her back to Kansas as quickly and painlessly as possible. At the very least he would maintain a strict client relationship with her, just as he had with Lorraine Kunin.

He could not get involved with Lizzie Olson!

To have come this far, only to fall for a woman from Wilson Creek! What a mess he—no, actually *she*—had gotten him into! There was only one way to get out of it—to keep her at arm's length and make sure they didn't get involved beyond the professional level. It would be tough going, but he'd start practicing right now, so he sat down by himself and ate the meal he'd hoped to share with Lizzie.

Lizzie returned to her room out of breath, not from shame or panic but from walking up six flights of stairs. She had been trying to fan the flames that were still soaring inside her. That was the best way to describe the feeling that lingered from her encounter with Michael: soaring, licking, hot flames. But the race upstairs hadn't helped. She peeled off her clothes, wig, and fingernails, and jumped into the shower. But not even the soothing spray of water on her sensitized skin could take her mind off Michael. Sensitive, charming, wonderful Michael.

"No!" she corrected herself. That *wasn't* Michael! The Michael who had kissed her would have thrown Lizzie Olson out on her ear. He'd been kissing Elisabeth Guest. He'd been sensitive, charming, and wonderful to *Elisabeth Guest*! He wouldn't have given the time of day to Lizzie Olson.

She had to remember: the suave, sophisticated New York designer she was pretending to be had never worked at Wolfe's Paint and Wallpaper in Wilson Creek, Kansas, and known Michael as a dark-haired and insensitive teenager.

Damn, she should have confessed everything and been done with it!

But he had given her such a beautiful out . . . and twenty thousand dollars, not to mention a new beginning and new hope. How could she have turned it down? For the sake of the truth? For trust? For honesty?

"Pshaw," she said, stepping out of the shower.

As she looked in the mirror, coming out her red locks and smiling at each of her freckles, she assured herself that she'd survive crossing Michael Wolfe. If nothing else, Mabel Wolfe would intervene and keep her son from killing poor little Lizzie Olson.

CHAPTER FIVE

Lizzie deposited Michael's check in the account for her fledgling business first thing in the morning and celebrated by treating Chelsea to brunch. They were dressed as themselves: redheaded Lizzie in wide-wale dark green corduroys and a cotton sweater, blond Chelsea in a jean skirt, striped pullover, and sneakers. If Michael walked into the restaurant, Lizzie figured that would be the end of Manhattan Interiors, Inc.

"No, no, I don't think so," Chelsea said as she poured maple syrup over a crisp, golden waffle, "I doubt anything would happen. He wouldn't recognize us."

"Want to make a bet?"

"Yeah, you're right. Knowing Michael, he'd smell our scent." Chelsea set down the syrup pitcher and looked unusually pensive. "Lizzie, he's going to find out sooner or later."

"Better later—after we've designed him such a smashing office that he won't care who we are."

"At least that much we're capable of. What are you going to do if he keeps coming on to you?"

"He won't," Lizzie said confidently. "I'm a minor and passing fancy."

Chelsea launched into her waffles. "Meg doesn't think so."

Lizzie paled. "Chelsea, please."

"Jonathan says Michael never had you out of his sight last night."

"He was probably afraid I'd steal a lamp."

"Did he kiss you, Lizzie?"

"Chelsea, for heaven's sake."

"Oh, terrific," Chelsea said, moaning. "Now we're done for. Conning him is one thing, but kissing—"

"Eat your waffles and be quiet."

For two bites Chelsea didn't talk. Finally she asked, "Did you kiss him back?"

Lizzie scowled. "Fifteen years ago that man told us all our taste was in our mouths. Would *I* kiss him back?"

"He was twenty-three then, Lizzie. People change."

"Michael may have changed outwardly, but inside he's still the same Michael Wolfe we knew back in the Wolfe's Paint and Wallpaper Supply Store days."

"Then why did you let him kiss you?"

"I didn't let him."

"You mean he took you by force?"

"No, by surprise."

Chelsea stabbed a chunk of waffle with her fork and popped it into her mouth. She looked as if she'd rather be nowhere else in the world than in New York eating waffles and hassling her best friend Lizzie. "I think it would be hysterical," she said, pausing to swallow, "if you and Michael got together."

"Chelsea, you're ruining my breakfast. If Michael's 'smitten' by anyone, it's Elisabeth Guest. And I am *not* Elisabeth Guest."

Chelsea shrugged. "So you keep insisting."

Lizzie changed the subject by perfunctorily ordering Chelsea to be at the offices of Michael Wolfe Associates that afternoon to finish the site measurements. Chelsea merely grinned. "Too chicken to show up yourself?"

"Not at all," Lizzie replied. "But you're my assistant, remember?"

"For this, Liz, I want blood."

"You may get it yet," Lizzie said dryly. "You can mop up after Michael's through with me if we don't pull this off."

"Ah ha. You know what I think, Lizzie?"

Lizzie turned over their bill and pulled out her wallet. "I'm sure you're going to tell me."

"I think you'd be a lot happier if Michael *were* an ogre. But he's not, and that's why you're so nervous."

"He is an ogre, and I'm not nervous."

"Then why are you leaving a ten-dollar tip?"

Scowling at Chelsea, Lizzie snatched back the ten and replaced it with a one.

When they returned to the hotel, they got down to business. They discussed possibilities for Michael's offices—colors, styles, uses of space, building codes, art, everything. Lizzie dug out sketch pads and catalogs and, for a while, forgot about regretting that she had kissed Michael back. Probably these things happened to him all the time, she thought, and he would think nothing of it. She had her work; she was good at it. Everything would be all right.

Having sent Chelsea off on errands, Lizzie skipped lunch and worked into the afternoon. Work had always been therapeutic for her: it had helped her through long, unsatisfying winters in Wilson Creek, through the early, uncertain years of her design business in Wichita, and now, through the nagging doubts about herself, Michael and her daring scheme. With her work she didn't feel so alone.

Just before five she received a panicked call from Chelsea. "Lizzie, he wants to come see you!"

"Michael?"

"Of *course* Michael!"

"But he can't. It's out of the question. Tell him I'm interviewing a client."

"I told him that. He says he has your address and is on his way."

"Chelsea, stop him! The address I gave him is of a Laundromat on West Seventy-second! Tell him he can meet me at . . . at the restaurant where we ate the other night."

Chelsea hung up and called back in two minutes. "He doesn't have time for dinner," she said, "he—"

"Guest, is that you?" Michael bellowed on an extension.

"I'm going to hang up now," Chelsea said, and did.

Lizzie cleared her throat. Even his voice gave her the jitters! But she managed to keep them out of her voice. "Is something wrong, Michael?"

"I reread that damned contract this morning."

"Did you?"

"Your letter said you could do everything for sixty

thousand dollars. The contract says a maximum of eighty thousand."

"Standard procedure, but I doubt it will come to that. I'm fairly sure that what I have in mind can be done for sixty—unless you want to get extravagant."

He said an unkind word. Lizzie smiled calmly. Maybe Chelsea was right. Maybe she was more comfortable when Michael was being a bastard.

"It also stipulates an hourly fee of forty-five for your assistant that *isn't* part of the eighty."

"True," she said.

"Damn it, woman, you're going to cost me a fortune!"

"I'm worth every cent, Mr. Wolfe."

There was an ominous silence, then sensually he murmured, "We'll see about that."

The line went dead. Lizzie wrinkled up her nose at the phone and went back to her drawing board. In the future she would have to watch her choice of words.

Chelsea crept in at six-thirty and collapsed on her bed. "That was slow torture," she said, then looked at Lizzie. "How come you're not dressed?"

"I thought I'd order some Chinese food and work through the evening. I'm on a roll."

"What about Michael?"

"What about him?"

"He told me—*Lizzie*! He's picking you up in half an hour."

"What do you mean? At the Seventy-second Street address I gave him? Chelsea!"

"He told me he'd worked it out with you. I thought—

79

oh, blast it all, I don't know what I thought. That conniving wheeler dealer."

"This is it," Lizzie said, capping her pen. "The end."

Chelsea sat up and pulled off her red wig. "Meg said to tell you not to give up, to trust your instincts. To persevere."

"Die fighting?"

"Something like that."

"Damn the man."

But in ten minutes she was in her black designer skirt, minus the jacket, and a cream-colored angora sweater that she actually owned as Lizzie Olson. She dabbed on what makeup she could, pulled on her wig, and dashed out the door. Michael was waiting inside the Laundromat, leaning against an avocado-colored washing machine. "Nice little place you have here," he said mildly.

"It's a mistake, this place. Your secretary typed the wrong address, but I know the owner and he brought the letter over to me. I forgot to tell you."

"Gwen never makes mistakes."

"Then I must have given you the wrong address at some point. Of course I don't live in a Laundromat!"

"Of course not."

She was breathless, her heart was pounding, and her nose flushed from both running and finding Michael looking so devastatingly sexy. He was dressed casually in cords and a pullover sweater. His arms were folded across his chest, the way they'd been the morning they'd met after not seeing each other in fifteen years.

"I'm sorry for the mix-up," she said tartly, "and I'm sorry I'm late. I was running a few errands."

"Then you are free for dinner?"

"Yes, as a matter of fact. Shall we go?"

"Don't you want to change into something more casual?" he inquired.

"No, I'm fine. Let's go, shall we?"

"I was thinking of a quiet, casual place. It's a nice night, don't you think? I'm not in any hurry. There's time for you to change."

"Michael, why do I get the feeling you don't believe me?"

He said nothing, merely looked wolfish.

"You think I gave you the wrong address on purpose, don't you? Well, I think Gwen simply hit the wrong key. This is ridiculous. A Laundromat!" she huffed. "I live in that building over there." She pointed, picking a nice one with a canopy. "Top floor. Really, I don't mind going like this."

For a moment Wolfe didn't move. He hadn't expected Lizzie to come right out and tell him where she was really living, but he was surprised to hear her lie quite so cleverly, which was foolish of him. She'd been lying smoothly and cleverly from the beginning. He was getting irritated—with himself and with her. One minute he wanted the charade to end so they could just be friends. The next minute he wanted it to go on and on so they could be more than just friends. Right now, however, he only wanted some assurance that Lizzie wasn't holed up in some unsafe part of town. What did she know about New York? He would have felt a lot better if he knew exactly where he could reach her, but he supposed he was being overprotective and underestimating her. She wasn't twelve anymore. From Wilson Creek or not, she was an adult, and she could take care of herself. He could push her, force her hand, but, for some reason he didn't quite understand, he didn't want to.

"Ever think of moving?" he asked.

"I've never met a New Yorker who doesn't."

"If you do," he said, "let me know. I hear about good apartments going up for rent every now and then. Let me know if you're interested."

Feeling positively benevolent, he hailed a cab. As Lizzie stepped in he noticed that she wasn't wearing her fake fingernails but he didn't comment on it. He simply climbed in beside her and sat close.

Tonight, he thought, *I'm not going to think about lies, charades, or Wilson Creek; I'm just going to enjoy myself.* "Relax," he told her, "I'm not mad anymore."

"Is this going to be a business meeting, Michael?"

He grinned. "I hope not."

She smiled back. "Why do I suddenly feel like a trapped canary?"

"Because you don't know me."

That, Lizzie thought as she leaned back against the seat, was an understatement. "You're right, Michael," she said, half to herself. "I don't know you at all."

They dined at a small, quiet restaurant on the second floor of a nineteenth-century town house in an older section of the city, which Lizzie would have known if she were Elisabeth Guest but didn't because she was Lizzie Olson. So she pretended to be familiar with it

82

and resisted asking touristy questions. Nevertheless, the restaurant was very elegant yet simple, intimate, filled with antiques, and Lizzie was hard-pressed to pretend that she was used to such places. New York wasn't better than Wichita, she insisted to herself, but it *was* different.

She wondered if Elisabeth Guest would have dined here before, but, noticing the soft gleam in Michael's eyes, she guessed that tonight it didn't matter. The setting, the quiet, the expression on Michael's angular face all invited a sharing of thoughts and hopes. If nothing else, a truce. He wouldn't ask about her Laundromat, and she wouldn't play too hard at being Elisabeth Guest.

But Michael was silent, and Lizzie was recalling the fourteen-year-old boy who had smashed her sister Hildie's Halloween pumpkin. Lizzie had gone after him with a half-dozen eggs. Had he changed? Had she?

She passed up a drink; he ordered a martini. She was determined not to be lured into a confession, but she was determined, too, to be herself.

"So, how long have you been in New York, Elisabeth?" Michael asked.

His tone was surprisingly brusque and businesslike, in contrast to the sedate ambience and Lizzie's expectations. She wasn't offended. Perhaps, as she was, Michael was fending off unwanted and inappropriate thoughts. She remembered the way they'd kissed last night. Undoubtedly he did too.

"A few years," she replied guiltily, wishing he had asked something—anything—else.

"Not a native, hm?"

She smiled, marveling at her calm. "No, are you?"

"No."

He smiled secretively as he spoke, and Lizzie wondered if he was thinking about Wilson Creek. Yes, probably. From the top of the mountain the poor folk in the valley always seemed so quaint and far away. He could afford to smile. For Michael Wilson Creek was only an amusing memory. Lizzie's calm dissipated. In her irritation she asked an unnecessarily direct question: "Where are you from?"

From the slight broadening of his smile she could see she had taken his bait. He wanted to tell her about himself, and she had paved the way by asking. In return she would have to tell him about herself. Knowing Michael, he would insist. And what did she have to hide? She began thinking up a past for herself and quickly flagged down their waiter and ordered a drink.

"A small town in Kansas," Michael replied. "You wouldn't know it."

"No, probably not. I never would have guessed Kansas, Michael."

He chuckled softly. "Not many would, but it was a long time ago."

Her blood boiled. "Thank God?"

His martini arrived, and he raised it in a mock toast and said, "Thank God."

That rankled, but Lizzie resisted a flip rejoinder. Elisabeth Guest would see his point. Definitely. Damn the man, she thought, and was glad when her martini arrived.

They ordered dinner: filet mignon for Michael; broiled salmon for Lizzie. Since he knew the restaurant and she didn't, she let him order appetizers. She hoped she wouldn't get indigestion. Chelsea would be disgusted with her boss for letting Michael Wolfe ruin a good meal, but Lizzie couldn't help it. It was strange, annoying, and undeniable that Michael could influence her mood. When she had sat at their linen-covered table, she had sensed possibilities of friendliness and intimacy. But all that was gone now. He was pooh-poohing Wilson Creek, and she didn't like it.

But she reminded herself that she couldn't appear irritated. Why would Elisabeth Guest care what Michael Wolfe thought of Kansas and his hometown?

"How 'bout you?" he was asking. "Where are you from?"

Tit for tat, she thought, and had her answer ready: "Chicago."

"Nice city," Michael said smoothly, but she noticed a slight narrowing of his dark eyes. "What made you leave?"

"I simply decided I wanted to be in New York," she replied.

"Yes, I can understand that. I left Kansas for pretty much the same reason—except Chicago has a hell of a lot more going for it than Wilson Creek ever did."

Seeing that she was about to squeeze her martini glass into several million pieces, Michael watched Lizzie set it down above her sterling silver spoon.

He was smiling mysteriously over the top of his glass. "Not many people know that little tidbit about me, you know."

"That you're from Kansas?"

"Mmm."

She shrugged. A magnificent act, she thought. What she wanted to do was to pour her martini down his shirt. Just what one would expect from a redheaded spitfire from Wilson Creek! "Why should anyone care?" she asked.

"This is New York, Elisabeth. Kansas is the Siberia of the United States."

"Excuse me, I need to use the ladies' room."

"Sure," he said, obviously enjoying himself.

Given her surroundings, her heels, and, most of all, the dark eyes following her, Lizzie did not stomp. But when she got to the ladies' room, she kicked off her shoes and paced. And paced some more. Then she tore off several paper towels, wadded them up, and threw them at the wall. Then she picked them up and—*zing, zing, zing*—popped them into the wastebasket. She was the only art teacher in the history of Wilson Creek High to have coached the girls' varsity basketball team.

She returned to the table, calmed.

"Are you all right?" Michael asked, seemingly concerned.

"Yes, of course."

Wolfe smiled to himself. He really didn't think Kansas was akin to Siberia, and he supposed he ought to be ashamed of himself for baiting Lizzie. But he wanted to know what she thought of Wilson Creek. Finally he was getting some hints.

"I think, Michael," she was saying, "that you're silly to be embarrassed about coming from Kansas. People are

86

people wherever you go, and Kansas is just as much a part of this country *and* this century as New York. In some ways I think it's more progressive. And the air's cleaner."

"I thought you were from Chicago."

"I am, but I've spent some time in Kansas." She gave him her most dazzling smile. "Hasn't everyone?"

"What part of Kansas?"

Damn, she thought, me and my big mouth! "Kansas City. I just love it."

"Of course." Michael finished the last of his drink. "Your auctions, I forgot. Ever been to Wilson Creek?"

"No, is it near Kansas City?"

"Farther west. It's a town in and of itself. It has farmers, one small factory, one doctor, one lawyer, and a nice little downtown. A lovely place."

"You don't sound very enthusiastic."

"It's that kind of town."

She took a big gulp of her martini, which she did not regret. Wilson Creek was not that kind of town! She had spent some of the best years of her life there. Yes, it was small, but so what? Wichita and Kansas City weren't far. Neither was Chicago, really. It was a fine place to call home!

Then why had she spent so many years plotting her exit? She sighed heavily, guiltily. At least Michael was honest. She had always wanted to live anywhere but Wilson Creek, not because she hated it, but because she had things to do and places to go. For generations Wilson Creek had offered everything most Olsons wanted out of life: good schools, a living, family, hope, a sensible life-style. A few had left, mostly for Wichita or Kansas City or another small town. But Lizzie had left for New York, New York. She thought of her sister Hildie and Jake Terwilliger and her mother. Their lives weren't easy, but they weren't unhappy. They thought Lizzie was missing so much by not being there in Wilson Creek with them, with a family of her own. Who was Michael to judge them? Who was she?

"Do you ever go back?" she asked.

"Not often, no."

"Then you have no family there?"

"My parents. They enjoy coming to New York."

"Yes, I can imagine," she said, and meant it. Mabel and Harold enjoyed going anywhere, but they always loved coming home. "They must be proud of you."

Michael shrugged. "I guess so, but they'd have been proud of me no matter what I'd done, including staying home and running the farm."

The farm! Why, you liar, Michael Wolfe! Lizzie coughed. "Farm? Really, you?"

"Uh-huh. Used to be up at dawn to milk the cows."

Michael Wolfe, of all people, didn't need to be told that there were no dairy farms in Wilson Creek. A few cows, yes, but that was it. "Your family runs a dairy farm?"

"Third generation on the land," he said, nodding. "But farming was never in my blood, I'm afraid."

That's for damned sure, Lizzie thought. "Who's running the place now?"

"My parents are, but I think they'll have to give the place up one of these days. I'm an only child, and, as

88

you can see, I have no plans to go back to Kansas. Me and the cows never did get along. But there are lots of people in town who'd be interested in our acreage."

"I suppose it's all for the best," she said, "but I'd hate to see my family have to give up their farm, especially after so many generations."

"There are farms in Chicago?"

"I'm speaking hypothetically," she said quickly.

He looked at her thoughtfully, but she avoided his eyes. They were the eyes of a high-powered agent, the eyes of a man who was used to seeing the things people were trying to hide. "You think I should go back to Wilson Creek and pick up the reins?" he said at length. "Become a farmer?"

"No, hardly," she said, managing an appalled little laugh. "But, as successful as you are, I would think you'd be able to help your parents out."

"How?"

"I don't know, maybe hire someone to run the place when they can't manage it any longer—so they won't have to see it go to strangers during their lifetime." Their place, she thought, which didn't exist!

Michael was shaking his head. "They've never asked for my help, Elisabeth."

"That's no reason not to offer it. It's not so awful to make sacrifices for the sake of family, is it?"

"Depends on what the sacrifices are and for what reasons they're being made."

Lizzie cringed and wondered what he thought of the sacrifices Lizzie Olson had made for her family.

"Families can be selfish and demanding—and loving

89

and kind. Some can be all those things at the same time."

He was serious now, talking quietly across the small table. A candle flickered, glowing against the shadows of his face and hair. Lizzie was mesmerized, her anger gone. She felt as if Michael were sharing some part of himself that was real and honest. He was lying about the cows and the farms, but she was lying about herself too.

"My parents wouldn't want me to give up my life and my happiness," he went on. "That would make them more miserable than selling the farm—and they like being independent. They don't like taking from their son, no matter how willingly I'd give."

Lizzie nodded, understanding more than he knew. Mabel and Harold Wolfe were content with their lot in life, although it was running a successful paint and wallpaper supply store, not milking cows. They worked hard, they loved Wilson Creek, they loved their son, they had enough to eat, a place to live, and, most of all, each other. That was all they wanted. When it came right down to it, Lizzie wondered, what more was there? She knew she desperately wanted to be a New York interior designer and knew she wasn't worried about bring thirty-one and not married, but she didn't know why. Why did she want to come to New York so badly? Why didn't marriage matter so much?

Because you've never met the right man. . . .

She looked at Michael, felt a wave of panic, and thought, *No, Lizzie, it's not him!*

She wanted to tell him about Lizzie Olson, the art

teacher at Wilson Creek High for so many years and find out if he thought her family had asked her sacrifice too much. Perhaps she had been too willing to make those sacrifices . . . or were they sacrifices at all? She wasn't sure anymore. She only knew that she was captivated by this bold and mysterious man . . . and wished he would say something nasty and ruthless so they could argue and she could play cool Elisabeth Guest.

But you are cool Elisabeth Guest! Or at least he thinks you are!

And Elisabeth Guest, she thought, wouldn't be caught dead in Wilson Creek, either. She smiled. "You're right," she said in Elisabeth's deep, sultry voice. "I can't imagine you on a Kansas farm."

That much was the truth!

Their appetizers arrived, and Michael gave Lizzie a big, happy grin that made her groan inwardly and remember the glorious feeling of being wrapped in his arms with his mouth caressing hers. "Tell me, Elisabeth," he said brightly, "has anyone ever told you that your eyes are the color of morning glories on a bright Kansas summer day?"

Lizzie looked up at him and stared into his eyes. "You know, don't you? Michael . . ."

CHAPTER SIX

Wolfe regretted his comment immediately. It was true: her eyes were the color of morning glories on a bright Kansas summer day. But he had told her that years ago, during one of his trips home from New York. She and Lucy Terwilliger had been designing their own line of wallpaper, and he had teased them mercilessly. The comment about the morning glories had been just another part of his barrage. As he recalled, she had taken it as an insult. He didn't think she would remember. But, obviously, she did. And he regretted opening his mouth. A confession from Lizzie now would ruin their evening.

"I know you're afraid to care for me, Elisabeth," he said, "but that's all I know. Try the pâté."

"But, Michael . . ."

"Blue eyes always remind me of morning glories. Eat."

Evidently she didn't need to be told twice, because she launched into her pâté like a martyr spared from the stake. Which was fine with him. He wanted her to remain Elisabeth Guest for a while longer. As he watched her eat he noticed her blunt, unpolished nails, bits of glue stuck in the cuticles, and paled visibly. It was all he could do to keep from chuckling aloud. Lizzie, Lizzie, he thought, where have you been all my life?

In Kansas, he thought, where you belong. . . .

"Something wrong?" he asked silkily when he saw her frowning.

"No, no, nothing," she answered as she put down her fork and tucked her fingernails out of his sight. "I . . . well, actually I was thinking about apartments."

He lifted his eyebrows. "I compliment you on the color of your eyes and you start thinking about apartments?"

"Yes, well, sometimes free association works that way," she said with a little laugh that didn't sound as carefree as she meant it to. "Anyway, Chelsea is looking. Her lease is up on her place. Do you know of an available apartment?"

"As of?"

"As of as soon as possible. This weekend, next." She gave a fetching smile. "She's threatening to move in with me."

"Engineer pants and all?"

Lizzie could have kicked him. "You never know with Chelsea."

"Pets?"

"No, none."

"Would she sublet?"

"Gladly."

Wolfe tried the pâté, savored it, watched Lizzie squirm. "I think I might know of a place."

"You're kidding! Chelsea will be thrilled. Where is it?"

"The place I have in mind is a one bedroom on the East Side, in the nineties."

With some effort Lizzie resisted asking how much the rent was. Elisabeth Guest would be able to guess, and the apartment was supposed to be for Chelsea. Michael didn't need to know that she and Chelsea would be splitting the rent. Unless it was a closet, a one-bedroom apartment would serve them nicely. Now that Lizzie had a contract with Wolfe Associates, she assumed Chelsea would be staying on in New York as her assistant.

"Sounds terrific," she said.

"Call me in the morning."

She grinned. "I'll do that, but I was hoping to see you tomorrow anyway. We need to discuss specifics about your space needs and some ideas I have."

"Elisabeth," Michael said, frowning, "how much of my time is all this going to require?"

"Tomorrow? Just an hour, I think."

"In my day an hour's a lot of time. What about all together?"

"You'll have to approve certain things, but certainly we won't have to see as much of each other as we have the past couple of days."

Even to herself she sounded disappointed.

"I didn't mean that the way it sounded," Michael said

94

softly. "Frankly I'd like to see as much of you as I can. But I'll be honest with you—"

"Michael, don't. You know I prefer to maintain a client-designer relationship."

"Do you? Some things you just can't help, Elisabeth. Me, I'm finding that it's damned hard to concentrate on my work when you're around."

From her point of view Lizzie couldn't agree more. "Michael, you're not at all what I expected," she said truthfully. "I'll try not to disrupt your life."

He laughed. Too late for that, he thought. The waiter brought their next course, and they ate.

Twice during dinner Lizzie almost told Michael everything. He was so nice, and she felt so guilty. But she held back. She wanted to enjoy him for a while longer as Elisabeth Guest, the woman he seemed to want and admire, not as the pariah from Wilson Creek.

"You look thoughtful," he said as they drank a strong after-dinner coffee. "A penny?"

"I was thinking sandalwood would be lovely for your reception area."

This was an outright lie. She had been thinking about the strange, wonderful ways the man across the table was upsetting her equilibrium and challenging her resolve to remain on a professional footing with him. She was thinking about his eyes, the finely tuned muscles in his hands and wrists, the easy blend of sophistication and earthiness that exuded from him. She was not thinking of sandalwood.

"Tan, you mean?"

She laughed. "Not exactly. But we can discuss it tomorrow."

"By all means," he said softly. "Elisabeth, I do believe you're as much of a workaholic as I am."

"I enjoy my work."

"Good."

She was watching his mouth and thinking how it would feel on hers. Tonight, she thought; yes, tonight. But then she realized what she was thinking, dreaming, and shook off the image just as if she were awakening from a very bad nightmare. She even shuddered. Had she actually considered going to bed with Michael Wolfe? It was impossible! Ludicrous! Suicidal!

Tempting. Oh, Lord, she thought, still watching him, was it tempting.

"My place isn't far from here," he was saying. "Why don't we walk?"

Lizzie started to decline but considered the alternative. If she insisted on going home straight away, Michael would hop into the cab with her and see her there. Then she would have to figure out a way of getting into a building to which she didn't have a key. Not a cheery prospect. And it would be all right to have a drink with Michael at his apartment. She didn't have to go to bed with him. He'd already proved that he was mature and sensitive and capable of accepting no for an answer. And she, of course, had proved that she was mature and strong and capable of giving no for an answer.

But all that was last night, and tonight was entirely different. . . .

"Sounds lovely," she heard herself saying.

Lizzie snatched the bill, but when she saw it, she wished she hadn't. Michael had expensive taste. She waited a discreet moment for him to protest, but he didn't. She was stuck. With unrivaled stoicism she counted out the appropriate number of twenties. It was better this way, she thought. She didn't want to feel as though she owed him anything. He was her client. He was Mabel and Harold's son. He was from Wilson Creek. They simply were not meant for each other.

She had just enough money left over for a cab from Michael's apartment to the Hotel Empire and tomorrow morning's breakfast.

Then she remembered the tip and forked over breakfast. It wasn't much of a tip, but she wasn't about to ask Michael for cab fare. Without a word Michael fished out a five and laid it on top of her ones. He took her arm as they left, and she half-unconsciously slid her hand into his, glad, in a way, that she had forgotten the false fingernails and didn't have to worry about them falling off. And what was wrong with holding hands with Michael? They were friends, weren't they?

But his skin felt warm against hers. His hand was so strong. She knew she needed him, wanted him, and it was foolish to try to pretend otherwise.

Nothing seemed more natural to Lizzie than walking with Michael Wolfe to his apartment, taking the elevator with him, laughing. They had both worked hard and were tired, but it felt good to be together. Inside,

Michael kept the lights dim and offered Lizzie a glass of sherry. She accepted, kicking off her shoes and curling her feet up under her on the couch. She couldn't take her eyes off Michael. He smiled, pouring the sherry into two small crystal glasses.

"Elisabeth," he said, walking toward her, "you know I'm not the type to beat around the bush."

She laughed. "Amen to that."

He sat beside her, handing her a glass. "Then I'm going to tell you straight out that I want you to stay here with me tonight." His voice was quiet and sensual, his eyes smoldering. Slowly but not at all tentatively, he reached out and touched her cheekbone with his fingertips. "I want to make love to you, Elisabeth. I've wanted to since I first met you."

"When I was measuring your ceiling?"

"Mmm. Somehow I think your masquerade of Chelsea had a lot to do with my initial attraction to you." He smiled devilishly. "The way her engineer pants filled you so well."

"Shame on you, Michael," she said, but she was laughing. He certainly was direct. But she had known that about him all along. The Michael Wolfe she'd known fifteen years ago in Wilson Creek had been just as direct. They were the same, that Michael and the very sensual man who was sitting next to her now. She lowered her eyes to her glass, then raised them back to him. "Why, Michael? Why do you want me to stay?"

He choked a little on his sherry in surprise but then laughed. "That's a hell of a question, Elisabeth."

Not a very sophisticated one, either, she thought, but she did not want to hear his answer. So she merely shrugged and tried to look curious, if not coy.

He touched her cheekbone again, trailing his fingertips down to the corner of her mouth and then across her lips. She could feel tiny sparks erupting all over her body. His smile seemed to touch her, and ignite her desire for him.

"Because," he said softly, "you intrigue me. Because I can't figure you out. I guess I've always been looking for a woman who has a little of Wilson Creek in her—oh, not that you've ever been to Wilson Creek. That's not the point. But you seem to understand who I am and where I come from. That means a lot to me, Elisabeth."

"But I—"

"I know. You're Chicago and New York. I don't understand it, either. Does it matter? Maybe we don't need to understand all that much. You're one hell of an attractive woman, Elisabeth, and—"

"Sophisticated?" Her voice cracked, betraying her heightened senses. And he'd hardly even touched her! He pulled his hand from her mouth, and she quickly sipped the sherry. *Maybe if I get drunk*, she thought. But she'd never been drunk in her life and didn't plan to start now. She'd handle her own problems . . . and her desires.

"Sure," he said, chuckling, "I think you're sophisticated—not that that's ever drawn me to a woman."

She smiled. "I don't believe you."

"It hasn't—not for long, anyway."

"What about the way I dress?"

"What about it? I don't give a damn about the way you dress."

Wolfe stuffed his smile into his sherry glass. He was telling the truth, at least part of it. He didn't give a damn about the way Lizzie dressed. He liked her in engineer pants, he liked her in designer dresses and slinky shoes. It just didn't matter. He wasn't sure why, but it didn't. At this point he wasn't sure about anything—except that he wanted her to stay. To hell with everything else. If her wig fell off during the throes of their lovemaking, that was just fine with him. He'd toss it on the floor and discuss it later.

I'm going mad, he thought, but he was incapable of doing anything at all about it. Or perhaps simply unwilling.

"I can't, Michael," Lizzie was mumbling.

"Can't what?"

"Spend the night with you. It just isn't possible. I never sleep with clients."

He twisted his mouth from one side to the other. She was worried about what he'd do when he found out about the wig and everything else. That she was Lizzie Olson from Kansas. Hadn't he hinted enough that none of that amounted to anything? That he didn't care? Or did he care? What would happen if he told her now that he'd known all along? That he'd recognized that prize Olson smile right from the start?

"Elisabeth," he began in a low growl, "Elisabeth, rules are made to be broken."

She shook her head adamantly. "Not mine."

He turned around on the couch, facing forward, and

put his feet up on his very expensive coffee table. Then he polished off the rest of the sherry and set the glass down hard on the table. He wasn't angry, he was frustrated. Every inch of his body aroused by the woman beside him. And he knew she wanted him too. He studied her out of the corner of his eye. Her fingers were trembling on her glass—not from nervousness, either—and she kept licking her lips. Seeing the tip of her pink tongue was driving him wild.

"Sometimes I think you're two entirely different people," he said carefully.

"Maybe because I am, maybe because we all are." She set her glass down beside his. "Thank you for the sherry, Michael—and everything."

"You're not going to tell me you're flattered, are you?"

She laughed because, for the lack of anything else, that was exactly what she had intended to tell him. "I am, you know."

"Do all your clients proposition you?"

"Only the handsome ones," she said lightly.

"Why, you . . ." Laughing, he swung one arm around her and dragged her to his chest. ". . . wise ass," he said with a growl, and kissed her hard.

But he caught her with her mouth open, ready to deliver a smart-aleck retort, and there was nothing he could do, or she, to prevent their kiss from deepening. Their tongues touched, wet and hot. Then she moaned, opening her mouth wider, and his tongue went in, stroking her teeth, probing and caressing her. Her arms tightened around him.

"Michael," she whispered, "don't say anything . . . please, not a word."

He didn't need to be told twice.

With a sexual hunger that drove him to the very edge of sanity, he slipped his hands under her angora sweater and felt the firm, warm skin of her waist. He kissed the corners of her mouth, the line of her jaw, the softness of her throat.

Lizzie fell back onto the couch, and Michael came with her, holding her, pressing his body against hers. She could feel his desire. Their eyes locked for an instant, and then she looked away. She didn't want to think. She only wanted to feel. To let the fiery desire in her body grow and grow and grow, and then be extinguished, quickly, in a burst of passion.

Slowly, with caring and intensity, his hands drew her sweater up. The coolness of his skin and the air of the room added to her sense of being on fire, of burning. Every sense was heightened, every millimeter of her skin anxious for his touch. She could feel her breasts throbbing with an ache that permeated all of her.

And after he'd gently unhooked the front of her bra they were exposed to the cool air, the touch of his hands, the warmth of his gaze. "You're beautiful," he murmured, "beautiful . . ."

"Michael!"

He was lowering his mouth to her breasts, and she knew that in a few moments they would reach the point of no return.

"I can't. . . ."

He froze at once. "What?"

She closed her eyes, fighting tears of frustration and a piercing sense of humiliation. How could she do this to him? How could she do this to herself? Stop . . . go on. Neither seemed right. There was too much deceit between them, too many conflicting emotions and desires within herself for her to make love to Michael Wolfe.

"I can't," she croaked.

Wolfe smiled tenderly, carefully, heroically, concealing his inward scream of sheer agony. She can't! The hell she can't! But he understood. He told himself, gravely, that he really did understand. "It's all right," he said in a hoarse whisper. "I can wait."

"No! I can't—not ever, Michael. Please, this mustn't happen again."

Bull, he thought, but said nothing. He fumbled at the clasp on her bra, finally got the thing fastened, pulled down her sweater, and rolled off her.

"It mustn't," she repeated.

He grabbed his empty sherry glass. "I can't make any promises."

"You have to!"

"Why?" He rose and almost started to laugh: her damned wig was askew. He chucked her under the chin. "I hate to break promises, and I can't stop wanting you just because you've asked me to. It just doesn't work like that. Now, do you want another drink before I take you home?"

"No . . . and there's no need to take me home." At least she wasn't so delirious as to forget that she didn't live on West-Seventy-Second Street! "I'll get a cab."

Wolfe slammed the glass down, nearly breaking it, forced a polite smile, and followed a suddenly brisk and purposeful Elisabeth Guest/Lizzie Olson out the door. Damn the woman, he thought. Tonight he was going to find out just exactly where she was holed up!

He got her a cab and then grabbed one for himself. "See that cab up there?" He told the driver, pointing. "Follow it. There's an extra ten in it if you can get me where it's going."

"Sure thing, bro'."

Wolfe felt like James Bond, except Bond never would have let Lizzie go in the first place. *I'm so damned honorable*, he thought, and huffed, aggravated.

His driver was good—dangerous but good. He followed Lizzie all the way to the Hotel Empire, across from Lincoln Center. A concert was letting out. Wolfe felt a little foolish, although damn little, that he hadn't granted Lizzie enough sense to have chosen a relatively safe and cheap place to live. He could just see her and Chelsea squirreled up there in one of the Empire's rooms.

He felt better. The driver asked if he wanted to get out, but Wolfe said no and headed back to his place. It was a cut or two above the Empire, he thought, but Lizzie sure as hell wasn't a gold digger. She could manage quite well on her own, damn her.

"Hell," Wolfe muttered to himself. "The more I curse her, the more I must be falling in love with her."

And that, of course, was the problem: He didn't want to fall in love with her.

Or did he?

Back in his apartment, he poured himself another glass of sherry and sat in his big, elegant living room and wondered if home had ever seemed so quiet and stark and lonely, and his soul so empty. He wished fervently that Lizzie had stayed.

CHAPTER SEVEN

Over a breakfast of muffins and coffee Lizzie told Chelsea nearly everything, neglecting to mention only the sherry and "et cetera" in Michael's apartment. Nevertheless Chelsea moaned and groaned about Lizzie's putting her head into the lion's mouth.

"Well, at least I have something on him now," Lizzie maintained. "He said he grew up on a dairy farm."

"Michael? A farmer!"

Chelsea burst into laughter. Lizzie started to laugh too. She had gone to bed feeling guilty and strangely unsatisfied, even lonely, and had awakened feeling the same. Now Chelsea's laughter cheered her up. Perhaps there was hope yet.

Abruptly Chelsea stopped laughing, took a huge gulp of coffee, set her chipped mug down, and sniffled at Lizzie. "He knows," she declared.

Lizzie knew instantly what her friend was talking about and scoffed. "Don't be ridiculous."

"I'm not. Lizzie, would Michael Wolfe have admitted

to Wilson Creek to Elisabeth Guest? She's supposed to be one-hundred percent urban and sultry and all that."

"He says he didn't understand why. . . ."

"Horse feathers. Would the Michael we know make up a story about being a farmer to impress a sophisticated New York designer he's trying to make the moves on? No way. Not our Michael. Lizzie, he knows."

"Impossible."

Chelsea shook her head with a self-confidence Lizzie found irritating. She took a gulp of coffee from her own chipped mug.

"Chelsea," Lizzie said, "if Michael knew I was Lizzie Olson from Wilson Creek, Kansas, he'd have tossed me out on my ear by now."

"You underestimate your charms, Lizzie."

"Michael Wolfe would never find any part of Lizzie Olson charming!"

"Why not? You find *him* charming—or at least sexy as hell."

Lizzie scowled and grabbed the bill. "No more, Chelsea," she said. "Not another word, do you hear? There is no romance between Michael Wolfe and Elisabeth Guest *or* Lizzie Olson. There won't be, there can't be, and I don't want to hear anything more about it. As for his knowing . . . well, he doesn't."

"Yes'm, boss lady."

"Oh, Chelsea!" Lizzie said, and laughed.

Miraculously Chelsea got them on the right crosstown bus as they headed to the office of Wolfe Associates. "Cheaper than taking cabs all the time," Chelsea said as Lizzie, dumbfounded, followed her into the crowded city bus. Chelsea grinned. "I can find my way around any city in the world, Liz."

Lizzie didn't doubt her for a moment.

Within the hour Chelsea was talking to Gwen and Michael's associates about what they wanted to see in their redesigned offices, and Michael was waving Lizzie into his office. He told whoever he was talking to that he'd get back to him as soon as possible and hung up the phone. He was dressed in gray, his white hair gleaming, and Lizzie thought he looked like the powerful literary agent he was. With the acidic coffee and doubt churning in her stomach, Lizzie suspected that she didn't look anything like the talented interior designer she was. She had put on a red silk dress, black stockings, and black shoes. She had even risen early to get her fake fingernails on right. She hoped Michael didn't notice that they were several centimeters longer than they were last night. *He's not a man for details*! But he was an agent. What were agents, if not people who noticed every tiny detail?

"Good morning," he said in a deliberately sexy voice.

I am not to think of this man as sexy, Lizzie admonished herself, managing a regal smile. "Good morning, Michael," she said. "I'll need just a few minutes of your time."

He spread out his arms, grinning. "I'm all yours."

"Yes, well."

She snapped her heels together. He didn't know. *Obviously* he didn't. This high-powered man would not waste his precious charms on a hometown woman. Forget it, Lizzie thought; he doesn't know.

"Shall we begin?" she suggested, her voice cool.

Wolfe got up and came around the desk. It was just ten o'clock, but he'd already sold a book and gone over three contracts. Of course, he'd come into the office at seven. He'd passed a bad night. He had dreamed of wheat fields and a red-haired woman with cornflower-blue eyes. There were moments when he couldn't tell if he was awake or asleep, nor did he want to. But work helped. It always did.

Lizzie smiled, and he remembered what a determined teenager she'd been. Sassy and silly but damned determined. He had always admired her for it.

He realized that she was telling him something about black marble and credenzas. "Whoa," he interrupted. "Don't you think we should sit down and go over this a little more slowly? Let's take our time. With the money this is all costing me I expect I'll have to live with what you come up with for a long time. Might as well like it, right?"

"Yes, of course. Where . . . you need a conference table, Michael. Really, for moments like this it would come in very handy."

"So you can add one to your plans."

"Yes, I was thinking we could include a small conference area in the third office. I—"

"For now can we use the couch?"

Lizzie was remembering what had happened last night on the couch in Michael's apartment. She couldn't afford to let something like that happen again. She didn't dare.

"I forget," Michael was saying, slyly, "you're allergic to fake leather."

109

"No, no . . . well, yes, but it'll be all right."

Licking her lips, she sat at the very edge of one corner of the couch. Wolfe sat right beside her, close. He simply couldn't resist. Lizzie's flush reassured him that he was doing right; it was not, he noted, a flush of embarrassment or awkwardness or any made-up allergy. She was just as attracted to him as he was to her.

"Elisabeth, you're thinking about last night, aren't you?"

"No, I'm thinking about a black marble coffee table and—"

"Elisabeth," he said, his voice a low warning.

"Michael, please."

She turned to him, her face tilted upward, and all he could do was smile and kiss her. "Don't turn me away," he murmured. "You want this as much as I do."

"Michael, I didn't come here for this—"

"I know."

He dragged his tongue along her full lower lip, felt her shudder as she closed her eyes and responded. He gathered her into his arms, and she came willingly, wrapping her arms around the hardness of his waist. He moved his palms upward, smoothing the soft silk of her dress until his thumbs were just under her breasts. With light, feathery circles he touched each nipple and, through the thin fabric, could feel their arousal. He opened his mouth, and she responded eagerly, wholly, and he growled with a longing he'd never known.

"We shouldn't," she said breathlessly between kisses.

"Why not?"

They kissed again, desperately, hungrily, and Wolfe

realized he'd been waiting for this moment, not just through the night but through his life. Damn, but she made him burn. She made him feel, want, and ache for her.

"We don't have to stay here," he rasped. "We can go somewhere else—"

"No!"

She leapt up, and at once he could see that she had come to her senses. She smoothed her dress and tried to ignore the evidence of just how much he made her burn too. Her wig was crooked, but she pushed it back into place just as she would have tucked back her own red locks, not even conscious of his enigmatic, knowing smile. She began to pace.

"The couch," she mumbled. "I guess I really am allergic to it . . . it makes me do things I shouldn't. . . . Oh, Michael!" She flew around at him and yelled, "How am I supposed to get anything done?"

Very calmly he leaned back against the couch and stretched out his legs, ignoring the evidence of his own arousal. Or at least pretending to. He was conscious indeed of how much he wanted to drag Lizzie Olson off to his apartment and make love to her for the rest of the day and into the night. Or lock the door and make love to her right there on the couch or the floor. He didn't care where, just so long as they culminated their ever-growing passion.

"Simple," he said in answer to her question. "Spend the night with me so we don't have this problem during the day."

She groaned. "That would only make it worse!"

"Yes, I suppose you're right." He grinned. "I have a feeling that once we get started we won't want to stop. Ever."

"Michael, that is not what I meant."

"Then what do you mean?"

"We don't know each other."

"Can't think of a better way of fixing that, can you?"

She sniffed, and he was reminded of her very upright mother, Hazel Olson. "I am not promiscuous."

He laughed delightedly. "No, darling, hardly. You are definitely not promiscuous."

Lizzie was already biting her lip, realizing that Elisabeth Guest would never have said anything so prudish and sanctimonious. "We have work to do, Michael," she said briskly. "I don't want to keep you any longer than is absolutely necessary."

"Ah," he said, his eyes dancing, alive, but his voice quiet and serious, "it's nice to want to do something besides work, don't you think?"

She grinned over at him, finding his mix of humor and seriousness impossible to resist. "Are you implying that you don't date women?"

"I 'date' lots of women, but I never become so obsessed with them that I neglect my work. But there's a first time for everything."

"Am I making you neglect your work?"

"Don't be coy, woman. I'm not complaining, am I?"

She shook her head, pursing her lips, which still felt swollen from his kisses.

"Elisabeth," he said dangerously, "you're not thinking about sandalwood again, are you?"

"Your lounge area," she corrected.

"Going to include a Hide-A-Bed?"

"Michael!" But a laugh bubbled over. "You're impossible."

"Just honest to a fault."

Ha, she thought, recalling his story about growing up on a dairy farm. Michael Wolfe had never milked a cow in his life, but, of course, Elisabeth Guest wouldn't know that. So she resisted inquiring further into his "mysterious" past and, with great self-restraint, suggested that they get down to business.

"Yes, ma'am," Michael said with remarkable humor.

Afterward they met Chelsea in the reception area. Later she and Lizzie would compare what Michael wanted for their offices and what they wanted and come up with a workable compromise. And, of course, Lizzie would have very firm ideas of her own.

"Lunch?" Michael suggested. "My treat."

Lizzie started to decline, but Chelsea, never one to turn down free food, accepted with glee.

"I'll take you over and show you the apartment afterward, if you have time."

"The apartment . . . you mean there *is* one available?" Chelsea appeared ready to jump up and down but didn't. "Great!"

Michael looked entirely too smug for Lizzie's taste, but there was nothing she could do but follow him and Chelsea to the expensive, elegant restaurant of his choice. If nothing else, she thought, she would gain a few pounds while fulfilling her contract with Michael.

"By the way, you two," Michael said shortly after

113

their meals arrived, "I've taken the liberty of referring Manhattan Interiors to one of my clients, Laura Gold. She's a vice-president of an investment firm on Wall Street and has done a damned good book on women in management. They've got about ten thousand square feet to be redone. She said for you to give her a buzz."

"Holy—"

Lizzie cut Chelsea off neatly. "I'll be sure to call her as soon as I can."

"Like this afternoon," Chelsea muttered.

"Of course," Lizzie said, "we're terribly busy."

Wolfe smiled to himself. He was feeling so damned benevolent. A regular Santa Claus. He paid for lunch and ushered the two women out. He thought about taking Lizzie's arm, but she looked a little icy. Chelsea had strands of blond hair poking out of her wig, down around her ears. Who the hell was she? A tall blonde, a friend of Lizzie's. . . .

"How long have you two known each other?" he asked idly as they walked to the corner to flag a cab.

To Lizzie's relief Chelsea let her field this one. "A few years."

"Is that right? Seems as though you've known each other forever."

Which was entirely true, Lizzie thought. "We've worked very closely, and obviously we have similar ideas about design. And we're good friends."

"You from New York, Chelsea?"

Chelsea nodded. "Queens, actually."

"You don't have a Queens accent."

"Of course not," Chelsea replied, as though that should

have been obvious. "I worked hard to get rid of it when I was eighteen. I spent a few years in London. By the way, where is this apartment?"

"The nineties. One of my clients rented it for a couple of months, but he's found another place." Actually Wolfe had arm-twisted him into giving up this apartment. "He likes to write in different places. One of his quirks."

"Jonathan McGavock?" Lizzie said.

"Yeah, Greening," Wolfe replied, using McGavock's more popular pseudonym. "Interesting character, and, fortunately, worth all the damned trouble he causes me."

Wolfe grinned when he actually saw Lizzie's spine stiffen. He was feeling more like the ruthless Michael Wolfe he knew, admired, and had cultivated over the years. Poor Lizzie was wondering whether she was going to be worth all the trouble she was causing him. Ha, well, how did he know? Maybe she was, maybe not. She was certainly adding a little interest to his week.

Oh, hell, who was he trying to kid? He hadn't felt this alive and happy in years. Maybe not ever. At least not since he'd caught Lizzie and her friend Lucille Terwilliger telling their Latin teacher that they were conjugating verbs between sales of paint and wallpaper and he'd—

Lucille Terwilliger!

His brow furrowed, Wolfe peered at Chelsea. Get rid of the red wig, add a full head of blond hair . . . *I'll be damned*, he thought. *I'll be damned to hell and back.*

115

Chelsea Barnard was Lucille Terwilliger! Wilson Creek was moving to New York!

"Something wrong, Michael?" Chelsea asked coolly.

"Nope," he said. "Nothing."

But Lizzie was licking her lips nervously.

They grabbed a cab and climbed in, and all the while Wolfe was thinking about the thousand and one things he would like to tell his scheming mother right now. But how in hell had Lucy become Chelsea Barnard? And how in hell those two ended up together in an interior design business?

"So how much is the rent?" Chelsea asked.

Wolfe had considered halving it, but he figured Chelsea and Lizzie would move in together and split it, anyway—and he'd only go so far with this Santa Claus act. Besides, if Lizzie found out, she'd accuse him of treating her like a kept woman. He had a feeling a lot of stubborn pride was sitting under that brunette wig. And, of course, if Lizzie and Chelsea had the gall to con an old family friend, they sure as hell could be real New Yorkers and pay their own rent.

"Nine hundred," he said curtly.

"A month?" This from Chelsea.

Wolfe said, "Yeah, I think it's fairly reasonable."

"I want a raise," Chelsea muttered.

"Don't be cheap, Chels," Lizzie said. "That's about what you're paying now, and you yourself have always said you want to be on the East Side. I think nine hundred is downright reasonable."

"No cockroaches?" Chelsea asked.

Wolfe laughed. "What a question from a born-and-bred New Yorker."

"Terrific," Chelsea grumbled. "Just so long as they're not bigger than I am."

Or me, Lizzie thought.

Chuckling to himself, Wolfe paid the driver—Lizzie forced a few crumpled ones into his hands, which Wolfe accepted with a growl—and climbed out. He pointed to the tidy, secure, seven-story building where McGavock had his latest hideout.

"It's gorgeous," Lizzie said. "Chelsea, this is your lucky day."

Wolfe did not mention that he'd gotten on the phone to his most famous client that very morning and practically booted him out of his own apartment. "You've got your penthouse on Park Avenue," he'd said. "You can hole up there for a while. I keep your wife so damned busy, she won't pester you. You'll find another place."

"Well, Wolfe," McGavock had said knowingly, "I've never known you to be so generous. Ms. Guest and Ms. Barnard have brought out your better nature, haven't they?"

"Who the hell said anything about them? I just know someone in need of a place to live, and since you're using a hunk of rare New York real estate six hours a day to type in—"

"Ten hours. I'm on a roll."

That had almost gotten Wolfe. McGavock "on a roll" meant he was nearly finished with his latest highly marketable masterpiece, which meant money to Wolfe. "I wouldn't think moving your typewriter to Park Avenue would make any damn difference," he said gruffly.

"At this point," McGavock had replied thoughtfully,

117

drawing out the suspense, "probably not. I was thinking of doing the rewrite at the orchard, anyway."

Being a forester and a sometime reclusive, independent woodsman, Jonathan McGavock also owned an
apple orchard in a quiet corner of Connecticut. "Great,"
Wolfe said, "then you'll be willing to sublet the
apartment?"

"Yeah, I guess. Meg always tells me you're a big
softie at heart."

Wolfe grunted. "She'll be out the door if she keeps
up that kind of talk."

But they both knew he was bluffing. Meg Oakes was
just as tenacious and hardheaded an agent as he was,
and Wolfe would be a fool to fire her. Besides which,
he didn't want to lose her very talented, if difficult,
husband as his premier client. Without mentioning Lizzie
or Chelsea, Wolfe made arrangements for Jonathan to
leave the key with the doorman so he could show the
apartment that afternoon.

Jonathan McGavock however, was waiting for them
when they arrived. "Ms. Guest, Ms. Barnard," he said
with a smirk at Wolfe, who was growling, "what a
pleasant surprise."

She and Chelsea smiled, said hello, and followed
Michael inside.

Jonathan was wearing jeans and a sweatshirt, a very
masculine, outdoorsy man, tall, well-built, a contrast to
Michael, who tended to assert himself more with his
strength of will, his searing honesty, his mix of urbanity
and earthiness.

In a way, Lizzie thought, it was like Chelsea and

118

herself. Chelsea was willowy and blond; Lizzie was small and redheaded. Chelsea asserted herself with her sense of being and purpose, undergirded by a nature that at heart was easygoing and noncompetitive. Lizzie was just different: flightier, more open about herself, more driven. Chelsea was content to be an "artist," whatever that meant, and to make ends meet as she could. Interior design as such meant nothing to her. One day she wanted to have a gallery opening of her paintings, but even that didn't matter. She was happy just to paint. Being successful at it—that is, making money—was inconsequential to her.

But, to Lizzie, interior design was everything. She loved her work, she loved the mathematical detail and the artistic whim of it, she loved the people and the success. She liked to make clients happy, she liked to make herself happy. And she liked to do a job well and get paid for it.

"We understand you're subletting your apartment," Lizzie said to Jonathan. "Chelsea is looking for a new place." She gave him and Michael her most dazzling smile. "Michael dragged me along to have a look too. I hope you don't feel as though you're being invaded."

Jonathan gave Wolfe another look. "Some things one gets used to. Here, let me show you around."

They weren't five seconds into the tour of the kitchen, a tiny alcove with down-size appliances, before Chelsea said. "Nine hundred a month and you don't even get a full-size stove?"

Lizzie promptly elbowed her in the stomach: Chelsea hadn't been reading *The New York Times* real estate section and didn't know a deal when she saw one. Chelsea coughed and changed her tune. "Amazing isn't it? I never can get used to New York prices, no matter how long I live here. The nerve! But it's a cute place. I'll take it."

"Wouldn't you like to see the rest?" Wolfe asked mildly.

Chelsea laughed. "Yeah, I guess. Why not?"

There was a dining area off the kitchen alcove, but Jonathan had it filled with an old oak table and stacks of papers. Wolfe was peering at a messy sheet on top of a ratty Yellow Pages, but Jonathan snatched it away and flipped it over, scowling at his agent. Wolfe merely shrugged. He was used to temperamental authors. Lizzie found herself laughing inside: she liked this big, hulking writer . . . and his imperturbable agent! If only she could be as hard to offend as Michael was. For years people had said that she was just too damned sensitive. "Got to toughen up," Chelsea—and others—always said.

The dining area opened out into a living room with an exposed brick wall, a fireplace that didn't work (Chelsea asked), high ceilings, and hardwood floors. Big, barred windows looked down onto the street. There was a love seat covered in brown corduroy, two wooden chairs, and a couple of orange crates for furniture.

"We can fix it up, can't we, Liz?" Chelsea said.

"I'd be glad to offer advice," Lizzie replied cautiously.

"Right," Chelsea agreed.

The bedroom was tiny and filled with books, papers, files, and certifiable junk. There was a desk with an old portable electric typewriter in the middle. Wolfe moseyed

120

over and had a look, but Jonathan said calmly, "I've already moved my manuscript back to Park Avenue."

"Is it any good?"

"I don't know yet."

"Always so damned closemouthed. No computer yet, I see."

"You're lucky I don't submit on stone tablets." Jonathan turned to the two women. "There's a twin bed in here somewhere. The sofa in the front room pulls out. You get the furniture, you know, such as it is."

Wolfe was shaking his head as he eyed the unprepossessing furnishings. "I make the man millions and he still prefers to work like a rat."

"You shouldn't talk," Lizzie countered, a bit too quickly. That was smart-ass Lizzie Olson talking, not cool Elisabeth Guest.

But Jonathan was delighted, and, Wolfe, grinning, smacked her playfully on her hind end. "That's why I hired you, isn't it?"

"One would hope," she said wryly.

Chelsea agreed to the sublease, thanked Jonathan, who said he'd be cleared out by tomorrow, and she, Lizzie, and Michael left.

Halfway down the four flights of stairs, realizing what he'd just done, Wolfe stopped and nearly threw himself over the landing. Benevolence wasn't getting him anywhere! Lizzie and Chelsea would move in together, split the rent, and set up shop and house in that meager little apartment. One would get the minuscule bedroom, the other the couch in the living room. There wouldn't be much privacy for either. And no room for would-be lovers.

121

He swore and stomped the rest of the way down the stairs. The two women pranced ahead of him, laughing and plotting. He swore some more.

He should have figured out some way to get Lizzie to stay in his apartment with him. Threatened her, even.

He banged open the foyer door. No. No and no and no. What he should have done was to have left the two of them alone. He should not have referred them to another client, one would could keep them in New York for weeks. He should not have gotten them a place to live.

He was helping them stay in New York, *not* forcing them back to Wichita.

What in the name of blue Hades was happening to him?

Was he falling for Lizzie Olson? An affair was one thing, falling for her was quite another. She was sexy and desirable, and he wanted to go to bed with her, but that wasn't the same as falling for her. Falling for her meant he couldn't imagine life without her.

He paused on a dusty step and thought about it.

It was true, he thought, he couldn't imagine life without her.

They were waiting for him in the foyer and grinning like two little tiger cats who had swallowed a couple of canaries. One named Michael Wolfe, the other named Jonathan McGavock.

"Thank you, Michael," Chelsea said, "you're getting me out of a difficult situation."

And me into a miserable one, he thought. "Sure," he said, not very graciously.

"Hurts to be nice, does it?" Lizzie commented, lingering beside him as Chelsea burst out the door into the street.

"Hurts like hell," he muttered, "hurts like hell."

When he hailed a cab, he politely opened the door and let Chelsea and then Lizzie climb in. He touched Lizzie on the curve of her hip. Suddenly he remembered how her soft breasts had felt, her mouth, her small, warm body pressed up against his. He began to sweat. He had an irrepressible urge to rip Lizzie's wig off and sweep her out of the taxi and tell her he was falling in love with her.

But he restrained himself. "You two go do what you've got to do," he said. "I've got a few things I need to get done while I'm in this neck of the woods. See you soon, okay?"

Lizzie gave him a big smile, and it was all he could do to shut the door on it and her and wave good-bye.

Then he went back to McGavock's apartment, asked his client to pour a couple of glasses of Scotch, and sat there and told him everything. Every damned word and feeling, just as Jonathan himself had done months ago when he had fallen hopelessly in love with Wolfe's newest associate.

Jonathan listened without interruption. Then, pouring his agent and friend another glass of Scotch, he said calmly, "Me, I'd have peeled that damned wig off the first night."

"You didn't tell Oakes you knew who she was." On Wolfe's orders Meg had gone to Connecticut to find McGavock, who hadn't sold a book in two years, had

123

written off Wolfe as his agent, and had claimed to have quit writing altogether. Wolfe, however, hated to lose profitable clients. Oakes had posed as an apple-picker or some damned thing. Wolfe was never too sure of the details. "You let her play things out for a while," he added.

"That was different."

Wolfe snorted.

Jonathan grinned. "Your little Lizzie doesn't make it as a brunette, Wolfe. She's a redhead all the way. I was wondering what didn't look right about her."

"Yank the wig?"

"Sure would get you two right out into the open, wouldn't it?"

Wolfe shook his head. "I'm not going to do it."

Jonathan refilled his own glass. "I didn't think you would." He raised his glass and offered a toast. "To scheming women."

Wolfe laughed, and they clinked glasses and drank.

CHAPTER EIGHT

Lizzie and Chelsea returned to the hotel to work, but all Chelsea wanted to do was talk about their new apartment. She rattled on about painting the walls peach and covering the love seat and putting up drapes—or maybe just colored blinds—and everything else Lizzie didn't want to hear about or talk about. Lizzie was glum.

"Does all this talk mean you've decided to stay in New York?" she asked sourly.

Chelsea folded her legs into a half-lotus and leaned against her headboard. "I couldn't in good conscience stick you with a rent like that. You'd go broke."

"So? I've been there before."

"Lizzie, Lizzie." Chelsea shook her head. "Guilt doesn't become you."

Lizzie sighed heavily. "He's been so nice."

"He has his reasons, I'm sure."

"I just can't keep deceiving him."

"It's a minor deception, Liz. Look at the big picture.

125

Look, what's the alternative? You want to risk returning him your 'seed' money? You already owe me from that last fiasco in Wichita. I know it wasn't your fault, but you can't go through life always being so damned honorable. You thought Wolfe would be suitable conning material, but he's not quite the louse you expected. Well, I ask you: What's the alternative?"

"I could just admit everything. And I don't see what's so honorable about conning him—"

"Guilt is usually self-indulgent, Lizzie. This is probably the first time in your life that you've put your own interests—minor that they are—above those of just about everyone else you know. If Michael doesn't understand, then to hell with him." Chelsea picked a piece of lint off her knee. "But I think he will understand. He likes you, Lizzie, and I think he knows a lot more about you than he lets on."

Lizzie flopped crosswise onto her bed, her feet dangling off one side, and sank her chin into her palms. "You think he knows I'm Lizzie Olson?"

"I'm not sure—it's a possibility. But that doesn't matter. He understands and likes *you*."

"You mean Elisabeth Guest."

"No, I mean you."

"You're a romantic, Chels. Michael isn't. He's a workaholic agent who's very good at looking after his own interests."

Chelsea lifted her eyebrows. "Is that a clumsy rationalization or what? What do you want him to be, Lizzie, a sleazy agent or a nice guy?"

"Oh, Chelsea, please! I'm too confused to think clearly."

"Too emotionally involved with our Michael to be rational, you mean. Look, he took us to lunch, he showed us an apartment—that's not the behavior of a workaholic. A workaholic would have left us on our own."

Lizzie groaned. "So whose side are you on? First you say I shouldn't tell Michael who I really am, and now you're telling me what a terrific man he is."

"He is who he is, Lizzie. What I'm saying is that it doesn't matter. Whatever he is, you can't tell him you're Lizzie Olson. At least not yet. Everything's going exactly as you planned, except that you're falling in love with Michael Wolfe and he's falling in love with you."

Lizzie's reply was a rude snort.

"Ha, so neither of you is willing to admit it. What do I care? We have an apartment, Lizzie. Freedom. Possibilities. Do you want to risk giving all that up?" Chelsea unfolded her long, slender legs and gave her friend a long look. "Now, are you going to call that VP, or am I?"

Without a word Lizzie sat up and reached for the phone. When she got Laura Gold, the vice-president Michael told her to call, she looked at Chelsea and said, "Ms. Barnard? This is Lizzie Olson of Manhattan Interiors."

Chelsea rolled off the bed and started beating on the floor.

"I understand Michael Wolfe recommended we talk," Lizzie went on, unperturbed.

"Yes, yes, of course," Laura Gold said. She had a clear, friendly voice. "He didn't leave me your name—just Manhattan Interiors. Lizzie Olson, is it?"

"Yes." Lizzie spelled it for her; Chelsea reached up, grabbed the pillow off her bed, and buried her head under it. "I thought perhaps we could arrange a meeting."

"Of course. I'm free next Wednesday. Shall we have lunch?"

They agreed to meet at her Wall Street office at one, and Lizzie rang off, feeling just fine.

Chelsea was glaring up at her from the floor. She had flipped onto her back and had her head resting on the pillow. "Go ahead," she said, "cook your own goose. See if I care."

Lizzie was running her thumb along her lower lip, thinking. "Chels, I think everything's going to work out just fine. I have a new plan."

Chelsea moaned.

Lizzie picked up the phone again and called Michael Wolfe Associates and asked for the man himself.

"I'm sorry," Gwen Duprey said, "but Mr. Wolfe is out of the office until Monday."

"Monday! Why? Is something wrong?"

"No, no, not at all. He left a message saying you were to have full access to the offices and that we were all to cooperate if there was anything you needed."

"Is he working at home? I have to reach him."

"I'm afraid he's unavailable, Ms. Guest. Mr. Wolfe has gone to Kansas for a few days. He said you would understand, which is very nice, because none of us does."

Lizzie's heart began to pound the way it had when she'd stood atop the bales of hay and waited for Michael to come reclaim his hill. "Yes," she said dully, "I understand."

"Liz?" Chelsea said, concerned.

"I will live through this," Lizzie replied, and dialed a familiar number in Wilson Creek, Kansas. Mabel Wolfe answered. "Mabel, please don't tell your son anything. I don't care what he suspects or what he knows, don't tell him anything. Please let me handle this."

"You mean . . . Lizzie, you need to know—"

"No! Just promise you won't say a word. Mabel, your son means a lot to me. I want to tell him everything myself."

"Lizzie, I think—"

"There's no need to worry. Everything's going just beautifully. Really."

When Lizzie hung up, Chelsea was pulling on her coat. "I'm glad I ate a big lunch," she said. "Because I have a feeling that's going to be my last good meal for a long, long time. I'm going out to have a talk with Meg. You want to come?"

"I should work on the space plans."

"What for? Looks to me like your days on the job are severely numbered. Come on, let's go."

Lizzie grabbed her coat. "We shall prevail, Chels," she said, and meant it.

Wolfe had expected three days of Kansas to cure him of Lizzie Olson. Spring was arriving slowly but beautifully in Wilson Creek. The air was clear and fresh, and the farmers were busy. He drove past the Olson farm and saw Hazel hanging white sheets on the line. He

129

met Hildie Terwilliger in the post office, and she invited Wolfe over to dinner. She was an attractive woman, like her sister, and wouldn't take no for an answer. So he went. His parents had refused to discuss Lizzie and Chelsea, but Hildie and Jake had no such inhibitions. They were a surprising couple: they collected folk art and ran their farm together, as a team, combining up-to-date technology with an old-fashioned love of the land. Wolfe was impressed.

And what he learned about Lizzie impressed him more, as well as unsettled him. After the death of her father Lizzie had seen her family through some tough times. This much Wolfe had known. He had assumed that those years had been miserable, wasted, but they weren't, at least not according to Hildie. Her older sister had enjoyed teaching and had worked hard to get Wilson Creek to understand and appreciate its artistic heritage. But everyone knew Lizzie would leave town as soon as she could. It wasn't so much that she had outgrown Wilson Creek as that she had what Hildie called "things to do." But, in the beginning, Wichita was as far as she got. She wanted to leave Kansas, but then again, she didn't want to.

"But, finally, push came to shove," Hildie said. "She had to leave."

"What do you mean?" Wolfe had asked.

"Well . . . I really shouldn't say. What happened wasn't her fault, but you know Lizzie. Her and her sense of duty. She took the blame, of course. But she's in New York now, getting a start there. You should look her up."

Wolfe we relieved to learn that neither Hildie nor Jake knew of Lizzie's little scam, but he was more anxious than ever to find out why Lizzie had packed her bags and moved to New York. Obviously something had gone wrong. He wanted to know what and why, and if there was anything he could do. He couldn't help it, he cared about her.

"Was she ever married?" he asked, wondering if it had been a man who'd prompted her to make a fresh start.

"Lizzie?" Hildie laughed. "No, not for lack of half the eligible men in town asking. I doubt she ever will, myself. She's practically a workaholic and . . . well, she'll probably stay in New York, and I just don't see her marrying a New Yorker. But you never know with Lizzie. She's happy."

Jake's older sister proved just as enigmatic. "Changed her name to Chelsea Barnard," Jake said disapprovingly. "Thought Ma would kill her. She and Lizzie make a hell of a team. Probably'll turn New York on its head, knowing those two. Remember when . . ."

And they had launched into a series of reminiscences Wolfe had found both disquieting and enchanting. These people remembered him as if he'd left Wilson Creek yesterday. And Lizzie and Chelsea and everyone else who'd come and gone over the years. The past was close to them, something they wanted to savor. That evening, when he'd left their amazing home, he stood along the fence to the side yard and looked across the Kansas plains. The wind was blowing hard, but the air was clear and bright and the stars were twinkling. He could see for miles.

Then he had gotten into his parents' car and driven home. Yes, he thought, home. For the first time in his life he didn't feel claustrophobic, hemmed in, trapped. He felt that this place was his. He wasn't coming back, not ever, but he, too, had his past.

Only he wanted it to remain his past. Or so he told himself over and over again during his remaining hours in Kansas and as he had flown back to New York. He didn't want Wilson Creek moving into his present in the form of one Lizzie Olson. As far as he was concerned she could finish up his office and walk out of his life to do as she pleased. He wasn't about to stop her, help her, or, God forbid, unveil her.

As long as she remained in New York, she was Elisabeth Guest to him.

But when he walked into his office on Monday morning and sat in his fake leather chair and looked at his slate blotter, all he could see were Lizzie's little feet, her red boys' sneakers, her engineer pants, her rounded bottom and dazzling smile.

And he knew he wasn't cured.

"There should be a vaccine against women like that," he growled, knowing he was irritated with himself, not Lizzie.

He was drafting a submission letter to an editor when she walked in. He even thought of her as "she," not Lizzie or Elisabeth, because she was neither, not really. The wig was gone, but in its place wasn't a bright blue polka-dotted bandana but her red hair—thick and gleaming with wispy curls framing her lovely face. The exotic designer clothes were gone, but there were no engineer pants. She wore a well-fitted navy wool suit, a white silk blouse with a narrow red scarf tied under the collar, and low-heeled walking shoes. Under her arm she carried a black leather portfolio. Her nails were short but not ragged, shining with a neutral polish. Her cheeks were peachy, her eyes bright, her lips coral and tempting.

Wolfe had half a mind to get up and kiss her, but since he wasn't sure exactly who she was going to claim to be this morning, he just sat.

"Good morning, Michael," she said cheerfully but a little breathlessly.

He put down his pencil. "Who the hell are you?"

She beamed. "You don't recognize me?"

Wondering why he tended to like people he couldn't even begin to intimidate, Wolfe picked up his pencil again and stood it up on the slate blotter, pressing the sharpened point into his index finger. Finally he said, "I'm not sure I want to."

She set her portfolio on the end of his desk, pulled up an ugly wooden chair, and sat down. She sniffled—buying time, he decided—and kept smoothing her skirt, which didn't need smoothing. She was nervous but not afraid.

"I'm your interior designer," she said, and smiled. "I've—um—changed since you saw me last. Sort of. Anyway, I have the space plans for your offices here with me. Chelsea and I were inspired between coats of paint this weekend and—"

133

"So she moved into McGavock's apartment?"

"Yes, we both did. I get the living room, she gets the bedroom. It's working out quite well, except that she wanted peach walls. Peach is all right but not for that apartment. Usually she's the one with the eye for color, but this time I prevailed."

Wolfe almost impaled his finger with the pencil, so he grabbed it by the middle, accidentally breaking it in two. Lizzie's eyes widened. This pleased him momentarily.

"We worked all weekend," she went on, her voice cracking here and there. "On the space plans and the apartment."

"What happened to West-Seventy-Second Street?"

"Oh, it's still there, I'm sure."

"I see. You've dyed your hair?"

"No, uh-huh."

He hesitated, not his usual style, and wondered what in hell he was supposed to say next. "Last week you had dark hair, didn't you?"

"Yes."

"What happened to it?"

"I sold it."

Wolfe didn't say a word. He simply picked up one half of the pencil and broke it in half, not accidentally.

"It was a wig, you see," she said.

"Why were you wearing a wig?"

"Oh, business reasons. You know."

Yes, unfortunately he did know, but he wasn't at all sure he wanted to tell Lizzie just how much he knew. Was she confessing—or not? Maybe she was just getting rid of the damned wig so they could make love without having to worry about it falling off. Well, that was all right with him.

He growled to himself: No, damn it, it wasn't all right with him!

"You see, my real name isn't Guest. The Elisabeth is correct—except you were right, most people do call me Lizzie. The Guest . . . well, I had a great-grandmother who was a Guest. She was from Wisconsin, but she moved to Kansas when she married my great-grandfather. He was an Olson."

"Olson?"

Wolfe forced himself to look surprised and suspicious, but he wished he knew he was taking the right approach. Why not just stop her now and tell her he'd known all along? Because, he thought, she might kill me. And he would hardly blame her. She was licking her peachy lips. Lord, but he wanted to kiss her!

"I thought you were from Chicago," he said.

"I've been to Chicago, but I've lived in Wichita the past few years."

"Not New York?"

"No." She shook her head several times, bolstering her courage. Then she leveled her cornflower-blue eyes at him and said, "I came to New York two weeks ago, Michael. I'm a very good interior designer but from Wichita, not New York. Put it together, Michael: My name is Lizzie Olson."

He picked up what remained of the sharpened end of the pencil and tapped it on the blotter. "As in—"

"As in the girl who used to work at Wolfe's Paint and

Wallpaper Supply Store in Wilson Creek and beat you at king of the hill?"

Pencil stub balanced under his index finger, jaw set hard, Wolfe stared at her, as if letting her news sink in. She sat with her feet flat on the floor and swallowed, as if waiting for the ax to fall. Wolfe let her wait. He would, if he hadn't known all along.

But she added in a clear, resonant voice, "I'm sorry I lied, Michael."

He didn't speak, and Lizzie began smoothing her skirt again. She would have given a great deal—probably a couple of toes, in fact—to know what he was thinking. Before she had left their apartment that morning, Chelsea had begged and pleaded for her to change her mind. But Lizzie had already sold her wig and wasn't backing down.

"Before you decide whether or not to fire me," she said, "I would like you to look at the space plans."

Michael's mouth twitched. She wasn't sure at all what that meant and was prepared for the worst. Then, with no other warning, he threw back his head and roared with laughter. Lizzie was even less prepared when he leapt out of his chair, bounded around his desk, and scooped her up into his arms.

"Michael!" she said, laughing too.

He smelled of a light masculine cologne, he felt of all the things she had dreamed of in a man: strength, kindness, laughter, hope. All the scents and feelings, all that she saw in his eyes and mouth and hair, all that he was combined and flooded her with emotion. With love. With a physical awareness that left her breathless. She wanted to make love with him—here, now, anytime.

But he merely smacked her once on the lips, hard, and released her. Just as he would have a long-lost buddy. "Lizzie Olson," he repeated wonderingly, chuckling. "I'll be damned."

Lizzie was offended. "You don't mind?"

"Well . . ." He pushed her portfolio aside and leaned against the edge of the desk. "Maybe you'd better explain the whys and wherefores of this little charade before I decide, hmm? In case you haven't forgotten, we did nearly spend a night together."

He said it as if that would have been anathema to him: making love to a woman from Wilson Creek. Lizzie was even more offended. "Frankly I wasn't sure you'd let someone from Wilson Creek touch your office," she said tartly.

"I probably wouldn't have," Wolfe admitted, fulling committed to his strategy now. "So you ran a con on me?"

"I wouldn't exactly call it a con."

"Ha! If you're not Elisabeth Guest, then you didn't work for Isaac Pearl, did you?"

"Well, no, I didn't, but I've done some top-notch work in Wichita and Kansas City."

Wolfe was relentless. "And the letter I supposedly wrote you?"

"I . . . um . . ." She blinked and looked at him without flinching. She would accept the consequences of her actions, regardless of what they might be. And curse Michael for looking so damned handsome while

137

he was interrogating her! "I'd like to tell you the truth, Michael."

He smiled. "And live?"

She smiled back. "That would be nice, yes."

He placed both hands at his sides, grasping the edge of the desk. "I'm listening."

"I made the letter up."

"Ah."

"I had tea with your mother one afternoon and slipped one of your letters into my purse while she was out of the room." She wouldn't implicate Mabel Wolfe. "She didn't know a thing."

Wolfe kept a grin off his angular face. "You're a shameless woman, Lizzie Olson."

"Yes, well, I suppose from your point of view I am, but I—"

"But you're a terrific designer."

"Yes."

"Shameless."

She did not look the least bit shameless. Or ashamed. Or even particularly embarrassed. Wolfe was pleased—and growing more aroused by the second. This third persona of Lizzie Olson was just as appealing as the other two. All rolled into one, they were downright irresistible.

He cleared his throat and stood up straight. "But I've been known to—ahem—use a few expedients myself from time to time." He grinned now. "I like you as a redhead, Liz."

She bounced up off her chair. "You mean, it's okay?"

He shrugged. "Let's say I won't call the Better Business Bureau. Now, let's have a look at those space plans. If they're no good—"

"You won't have to fire me. I'll leave on my own accord."

"Sounds fair enough."

She grinned, delighted. "Oh, Michael!"

"Now don't start treating me like St. Francis, because I'm not. You're going to be held to your contract, woman. I want good work out of you. Charity is not my strong suit—at least not for people who don't deserve it."

"I don't want charity, Michael," she said sharply. "That, more than anything, was why I came to you as Elisabeth Guest. Your parents helped me out when I was in high school, but I worked hard for them. Still, that's enough. I want to become successful on my own merit."

He raised his eyebrows, resisting the softness of her mouth. She was so serious. But still he couldn't kiss her now. He had to give himself time to adjust to her "news." *Then* he would go after her. He couldn't wait.

"Your merit, Lizzie, or Elisabeth Guest's?"

"She's me, Michael," Lizzie said quietly, her face grave and unsmiling, her mood shifting yet again. Michael was being nice enough, but did she want nice? Maybe a little ranting and raving would have been better. It would have meant, at least, that Elisabeth Guest had meant something to him. "I'm just as talented and knowledgeable as she is."

"And if you measure up, then we still have a contract. If not—"

"I'll measure up," she said stiffly.

Wolfe gave her a long look, seeing her anger, and yes, her frustration. He wasn't reacting the way she wanted him to react. Well, good, he thought. They had a lot to sort out, him and lovely Lizzie. "Irritated?" he asked softly.

"No, why should I be? You're the one who should be irritated."

Ah, he thought, so that was it. "You thought I'd yell and scream?"

She reared back her shoulders. "That does seem to be your style."

"Ah ha, I see," he said musingly. "Maybe we'd better wait to go over the space plans. Easy—don't get excited." He handed her her portfolio. "Go home. Relax."

"But, Michael, the space plans . . ."

"Give me some time, Lizzie. If you think I can concentrate on space plans right now, you're underestimating everything that went on between us last week."

"You mean. . . ."

"I don't know what I mean. Give me a chance to find out, okay? Look, come to my apartment tonight—six o'clock. We can discuss space plans then." He grinned. "Or not."

Her chin shot up, and he could see the life in her eyes, the hope, and he smiled to himself. She tucked her portfolio under her arm, promised she would be at his place at six o'clock sharp, and darted out.

Wolfe made sure she was gone before he bounded out to Gwen and told her he was going out for half an hour for a round of squash.

"Squash? At ten o'clock in the morning?"

He growled a yes as he left. Thirty minutes might not do it, but he had to give it a try or the frustration of not having kissed the stuffing out of a certain redhead was going to drive him mad.

CHAPTER NINE

Lizzie stomped into Meg's office, said hello, grabbed Chelsea, who had come to work as the gorgeous blonde she was, and dragged her into a coffee shop for a cup of coffee. Lizzie told her everything, concluding with, "I can't stand it, the man is going to drive me crazy!"

But, as always, Chelsea put events into perspective. She flipped back her gleaming blond locks and said, "Well, at least you're alive to tell me about it."

"He called me shameless."

"If the shoe fits . . ."

"He seemed . . . different."

"You're Lizzie Olson from Wilson Creek now, not Ms. Elegant Guest. You're looking at each other from a new perspective."

"I've always known who I am—and who he is."

Chelsea shrugged. "We shall see."

"We shall not see. I'm just going to do my job and forget everything else."

"Sure."

142

"I am!"

"Ah, romance," Chelsea said with a magnificent grin.

"Romance! I'm ready to murder that man!"

"Not so loud, this is New York. Someone might take you seriously." But Chelsea was suppressing a grin. "You're just mad because Michael was nice and didn't throw you out on your ear the minute he found out who you really are. You thought the moves he was making on Elisabeth Guest were part of an act—not the real, obnoxious Michael Wolfe you've always known. But it wasn't an act. Michael is the same good-looking, interesting, ruthless, sensitive man he was last week, and that makes you nervous."

"It does not."

"Fiddlesticks. Lizzie, you're in love."

"Give me a break."

"Actually I should think Michael would be relieved to find someone who can love him for all the things he is—miserable cur included. He doesn't have to put on any shows for you, Lizzie. You know what and who he is. And vice versa."

Lizzie frowned at her friend. "Chelsea, I couldn't possibly be in love with Michael Wolfe. It gives me the heebie-jeebies just thinking about it."

"I've known you thirty-one years, Lizzie Olson, and I've never seen you act like this." Chelsea peered at something disgusting stuck to the rim of her coffee mug, then shrugged. "Guess whatever it is belongs."

"Chelsea, please," Lizzie said, groaning. "How can you be so—so calm?"

"Because I'm not the one in love."

At five o'clock Lizzie decided she wasn't going to meet Michael at his apartment that evening. No way, no how. She would call and tell him she was busy and would see him tomorrow. At the office. Preferably with the door open. Preferably with Chelsea at her side.

Meeting him at his apartment was just asking for trouble.

But she wanted to get his reaction to the space plans. What if he didn't like them? What if there was a problem? What if he was going to bounce her off the project?

"Back to Wichita in ignominy," she muttered, staring down at the street below her new apartment. It was a nice street, a nice apartment. Cozy, New York. She loved the city. She really did. But she loved Kansas too. It wouldn't be so bad to go back. "But not in ignominy."

She hated having Michael in control now. He was calling the shots. He had her head on the guillotine, and he could chop it off if he wanted to. She was just little ol' Lizzie Olson who used to sell wallpaper and teach art and conjugate Latin verbs better than anyone at Wilson Creek High.

A damned hayseed, Michael would say.

Well, so was he!

It was gloomy out, chilly. Lizzie put on a pair of double-pleated navy cords, a cotton oxford shirt, and a gold cotton crewneck sweater. Loafers. Knee socks. No makeup. Her hair was still rejoicing at its newfound freedom, so she just combed it and let it do as it pleased. Mostly it just hung there. But she looked presentable: like herself, not Elisabeth Guest or any facsimile thereof. Just herself.

And Michael could take her or leave her.

This time she noticed details about his building she hadn't noticed before. There were mirrors in the lobby, which was bigger than her apartment, and the night doorman was excessively polite. There was an elevator—more mirrors—and halls with cream-colored walls and thick carpets. Lizzie had never taken anything more than a professional interest in such trimmings. Her own life didn't have to be filled with glamor and expensive objects. That, she thought, was her Wilson Creek heritage. And she was damned proud of it.

Michael let her in. If she could have, she would have turned right around and walked out again without a word. He was wearing dark gray slacks and a cashmere pullover and holding a martini. His eyes grabbed her and held her. Her breath caught. She could never be neutral about this man. It would be much simpler just to leave, but she couldn't. Everything about him willed her to stay, but that was only part of the problem: She wanted to stay. It would be simpler to leave, but leaving was impossible.

"Can I fix you a martini?" he asked in his silkiest, deepest voice.

"No, I hate martinis."

He laughed. "Glad to be Lizzie Olson again?"

"Yes."

"Still irritated?"

"No."

She pulled off her jacket, but he caught it just as it

145

was at her elbows and said, his breath warm on her ear, "Here, allow me."

Since she had no choice in the matter, she allowed him. Every move, every sound he made struck her in the oddest places, which she hadn't expected at all. She had thought, somehow, that becoming Lizzie Olson would change how she felt about Michael Wolfe. How she reacted to him. Lizzie Olson wouldn't find him so sensual.

She had been wrong, of course. If anything, the absence of the awkward wig and the long, fake fingernails made her more conscious of the rest of her, the parts of her that were aching for his touch.

Yes, that was it: his touch. Might as well be honest about it, she thought. Nothing had changed. She still wanted to make love with Michael Wolfe. And that irked her.

He hung up her coat, closing the closet door softly. "And what does Lizzie Olson drink?"

"Scotch," she said, "on the rocks." It was the truth.

He was amused, which further soured her mood. What did he expect Lizzie Olson to drink? A sloe gin fizz? Ginger ale? She followed him into the living room and decided she might as well ask and be just as sarcastic about it as she pleased. So she did.

Michael appeared remarkably unperturbed, even amused. "Actually I don't know."

"But you're surprised I drink Scotch."

"Yes, I suppose I am. Does that bother you?"

She skirted his question by asking one of her own. "Why shouldn't I drink Scotch?"

146

"No reason you shouldn't. I've never objected to anyone having an occasional drink—myself included."

He went into the kichen, got a glass out of a cupboard and ice out of the freezer—just like a normal person—and returned to the living room. He poured the Scotch from a crystal decanter.

"Back in Kansas," Lizzie said perversely, "I keep my Scotch in a bottle under the sink."

"Next to the Drāno?"

"Who could tell the difference?"

He handed her the glass—she noticed that his fingers were warm and steady—and watched her take a sip. She wondered if he expected her to gag. Damn him. But Scotch was indeed her drink, although she didn't in fact keep a bottle under her sink or even in her apartment.

Nevertheless she could manage quite a swig without so much as a tiny cough. Not very nice but effective. Michael's eyes widened, and then he smiled. The smile brought a pleasant quiver to her back, which she wanted to ignore but couldn't. She almost took another gulp but changed her mind. Getting tipsy wouldn't help anything. She sat down instead and wished she had worn her engineer pants. That would have given him a start.

"So tell me, Lizzie," he said casually, sitting sideways beside her on the couch and drawing one knee up under him. He paused, sipping his martini, but his eyes never left her. "Why are you acting like a little jerk?"

Of course, he was right. She *was* acting like a jerk.

But he was smiling and looking so damned in control, which didn't foster any incipient feelings of remorse. "Because I am a little jerk," she snapped.

"As I recall," he said, laughing, "you were."

"Me!"

"Yes, you."

"*You* were the jerk!"

He laughed, the corners of his eyes crinkling. "Was I?"

"Arrogant, nasty, wise-assed—"

He leaned forward. "Darkly handsome."

"Serves you right for going white."

"Makes people think me even more arrogant, nasty, and wise-assed than I am. You have your red hair."

"For what?"

"For making people think you're more arrogant, nasty, and wise-assed than you are."

She sniffed. "I am none of those things."

"I beg to differ, Ms. Olson. Remember, I'm the man you've been conning for the past week."

" 'Conning' is a bit strong, Michael."

"Did I or did I not hand you a check for twenty thousand dollars?"

"You'll get your money's worth."

"You're damned right I will."

He finished his martini, and she worked furiously on her Scotch. She wasn't certain what he meant by that last comment, especially since it was delivered in his most unbusinesslike, un-Wolfe-like, silkiest voice. The voice that made her want to melt.

"If I had really conned you," she said, "I would have skipped town with the twenty grand."

"And I'd have followed you to hell and back, Lizzie, dear."

Yes, he certainly would have. "But you'd never have known to look for Lizzie Olson."

"I'd have found out."

"Well, I didn't go, did I?"

"No, you didn't." He stretched his arm across the back of the couch, until his fingers touched her hair. "Don't be angry with me because you decided to tell the truth, Lizzie."

"I'm not angry with you!"

But she spoke heatedly and knew he was right. She was angry but not at him. At herself. If only she hadn't judged him before she saw him. If she only had believed Mabel Wolfe when she had said how charming her son was. Fifteen years had changed him. And her. She turned away, putting her feet flat on the floor and stretching out her legs. After a long, cathartic sigh she looked over at Michael, whose hand was still at the back of her head, and said, "Shall we go over the space plans?"

He smiled. "As you wish."

She got out her portfolio and handed the plans over to Michael. She had penciled in the layout for all six offices. If Michael approved, she would complete the final color board.

He glanced at them, then handed them back to her. "They're fine."

Usually she had to go over points, make explanations, argue this or that. Clients rarely glanced at something that was going to cost them thousand of dollars and dismissed it so quickly. "Fine?" she said.

"Rather good, in fact."

"How could you tell?"

"I can tell. You want a detailed compliment? All right. You've taken everything my associates told you and everything I told you and come up with workable compromises. You found space in each office for a private consultation area. That's good. You obviously understand that we don't get much foot-traffic and therefore can use the reception area for more than just receiving people—storage, conferences. I like that. But the important thing was to give us all the feel of airiness and comfort when we work. Most of what we do is over the phone and through the mails, but it's a busy, intense office. So. Very good, I like it."

"Just like that?"

"Just like that. Of course, I understand this is only the beginning. I look forward to seeing your final plans."

"Well, then, thank you. I'll get started on the color board right now." She smiled over at him. "This is the quickest business meeting I've ever had. Thanks, Michael."

He watched her put the plans back into her portfolio and couldn't believe she was actually going to get up and leave. But, yes, she was. She smiled at him, got up and put out her hand. Indeed, the woman was going to shake hands with him and depart into the night.

But not if he had anything to say about it.

He did take her hand. "Leaving?" he murmured.

"Yes, unless there's anything else—"

"There's everything else."

"What?"

"You know what, Lizzie."

"Michael, I'm willing to forget last week. I understand. You thought I was someone else. Now that I'm Lizzie Olson from Wilson Creek—"

He still held on to her hand. "That hasn't changed anything."

"What do you mean?"

He laughed softly and drew her down beside him. She could have run—he wasn't a cad, he would have let her—but she didn't. She sat close, her thighs touching his. Her eyes were big and round but not innocent. She knew what he meant.

He simply said, "Stay."

"Michael, are you sure?"

"I've been sure, Lizzie. I've wanted to make love with you from the minute I saw you."

"But I was Elisabeth Guest then."

"No, you weren't. You were Lizzie Olson—standing on my desk, remember? Or Chelsea or whoever. It doesn't matter."

"It does matter," she said in frustration, placing her hand on his. "Michael, I'm from Wilson Creek."

"So?"

"So I know you're not a farmer."

He laughed. "I was pulling your strings, Lizzie. I've never told anyone that particular lie."

"But why me?"

"Who knows?"

He lifted her hand and pressed it to his lips, not politely or cavalierly, but very, very sensually. Lizzie drew in a sharp breath.

"You've always been Lizzie Olson," he said.

"Lizzie Olson doesn't drink martinis."

"She drinks Scotch. She could drink ginger ale and I wouldn't care."

"Wouldn't you? Don't you?" She pulled her hand away. "I remember the things you said about Wilson Creek, Michael. That's my hometown. You can't make me into Elisabeth Guest. I'm—"

"Lizzie Olson," he finished, forcing himself to remain patient. "Wilson Creek is my hometown, too, Lizzie."

"*Now* it's okay."

"It was always okay. I just don't want to live there."

"You called it hell on earth."

"Did I?" He laughed. "Yeah, I probably did. I think we all did at one time or another—even you."

"Never."

"Ha. Look, Lizzie, I told you: I've been waiting for a woman who's a little Wilson Creek and a little New York. That's you."

"I am not a little New York."

"Sure you are—but mostly you're just yourself."

Placing her palms on her knees, she turned away. "Elisabeth Guest was an act, Michael."

"I don't believe that, not entirely," he said quietly. "You can't pretend you're a Wilson Creek girl who's never wanted anything but a home and a bunch of kids on the family farm. And I can't pretend I've never stepped foot in Wilson Creek and haven't wanted those things too. Don't feel guilty because you wanted to leave, Lizzie. Wilson Creek will always be home. Nothing's going to change that. Believe me, I know. But you can't go back, and neither can I."

She refused to look at him and said stubbornly, "I can."

"No, not even if you wanted to, not permanently." He sighed, his patience gone. "Lizzie, I'm going to give you three seconds to make up your mind. After that I'm going to kiss you—and you and I both know what that will lead to. If you want to go, go now. But don't think that'll be the end of it, because it won't. You mean too damned much to me. I don't intend to give up just because you feel guilty—"

She flew around at him. "I do not feel guilty!"

He grinned. "Struck a chord, did I? One."

"Michael, damn it, I don't like ultimatums!"

"Two."

"You can stuff your three seconds."

"Three."

She was still there. She knew she would be. Her arms were crossed against her chest; her feet were stretched out. She was in a royal huff. But Michael didn't seem to care. He took her by the waist, turned her toward him, and saw the glint in her eye, the smile she was fighting.

"You devil," he said, and kissed her.

Michael's bedroom was airy and masculine, not heavy or dark. That wouldn't have been Lorraine Kunin's style, or his. Lizzie was about to tell him this, but he informed her, huskily, slipping his arms around her waist from behind, that if she commented on the decor, he was going to pitch her out the window.

"That's what I like about you, Michael," she said with a laugh. "You never mince words."

"Never have."

"This is true. I can remember when you were sixteen and—"

"Stories about my youth gets ice down your back."

"Ha! I'd like to see that! Remember, Mr. Wolfe, I'm the one who routed you at King of the Hill every time."

His hands edged up her midriff and stopped just below her breasts. "I let you win."

"You never let anyone win at anything in your life!"

"You were a chubby little pain in the neck with braces and pigtails—"

"All the more reason not to let me win."

"My mother said I shouldn't browbeat little kids."

To this Lizzie had no quick comeback. "All right, Michael," she said, "I won't tell stories about your youth if you won't tell stories about mine." She tilted her head back and looked up at him. "Chubby little pain in the neck, huh?"

He grinned. "But cute. As I said, we've both changed."

"Meaning?"

"Meaning . . . *hi-ya!*"

With not exactly blinding speed she elbowed him in the abdomen, which undoubtedly hurt her more than it hurt him. He laughed and called her a maniac. His grip on her stomach did not loosen appreciably. She butted him with her bottom.

"Oh," he said, "I like that."

She pretended to be horrified and whirled around inside his arms. He wasn't that much taller than she

154

was, but he was wiry and strong, and she could feel the muscles in his arms tightening. She raised both her arms, then smashed them down onto his. Instead of breaking his hold on her, she only managed to clamp herself firmly against him. Her breasts strained against his hard chest. His hands were folded around the middle of her back.

"Of course, I planned it that way," she said.

"Of course."

"I could get out if I wanted to."

"You could."

"I took a night course in self-defense at Wichita State."

His dark eyes were laughing. "And against what are you defending yourself, Ms. Olson?"

"A miserable cur who—"

"Miserable cur?"

She laughed. "Chelsea's phrases. She's really Lucille Terwilliger, by the way. She changed her name to Chelsea Barnard ten years ago because she didn't like the way the British pronounced Lucille Terwilliger. You remember Lucy, don't you?"

"Indeed. You both held Wolfe's Paint and Wallpaper hostage for two interminable years. Still friends after all this time?"

"And why not? It's nice to have someone close to you who shares your roots, knows your past."

He smiled tenderly. "Yes, it certainly is."

Michael leaned forward, causing Lizzie to lose her balance and start to fall. He didn't steady her, nor did his grip loosen. He just held on tight and fell with her.

They landed comfortably, easily, cushioned by the stark-white comforter on his king-size bed.

"No more talk," Lizzie said. "Please."

Her arms were around his neck. She smiled into his eyes and plucked at the ends of his hair with her fingers. The skin at the back of his neck was warm. Gently she pressed down, urging him toward her. He smiled then, and their mouths came together, slowly, hungrily. She felt his chest expand as he inhaled.

He slid his arms out from under her and placed them on the comforter, beside her shoulders, lifting his torso off her, so just their mouths and hips were joined. He moved his hips, ever so slightly but ever so erotically. Lizzie's thighs parted, and he settled in there, moving, moving. And all the while his tongue moved within her mouth in that same slow, pulsing rhythm.

"No more talk," he agreed, his voice little more than a gentle growl.

She wasn't sure, even then, whether she slipped her hands under his shirt first or if he slipped his hands under her shirt first. She was only aware of the warmth of his skin beneath her hands, its coolness on her stomach, and then the ache that spread through her.

"I'm not very good with the layered look," he muttered. "Unless you don't mind losing a few buttons . . ."

She laughed, sitting up as he rolled off her. Side by side they undressed. There was built-up passion in the air, a near-tangible sexual electricity, but there was something else too. Something Lizzie had never experienced in her thirty-one years. She couldn't quite describe the feeling, but it was there. This was their first time together like this, and yet it seemed as though it wasn't. The silence between them was filled with promise and passion, but it was companionable too.

"You feel it, too, don't you?" Michael said.

"Yes, but I don't know what it is. It's sort of . . . I don't know. It's as though I've known you—"

"All your life?" he finished.

Lizzie laughed. "Yes, that must be it."

"Can't imagine why," he said, and removed his shirt.

His chest was taut and covered with dark hairs. Lizzie paused to look at every one of them, but he urged her on, warning her that he did keep a needle and thread about. Without a thought she whisked off her shirt and bra, depositing them on the floor.

It was Michael's turn to pause and stare. "You are beautiful," he said.

Her breasts were full and round, with peachy-pink nipples. He nodded at their already aroused state. "It's the cool air," she insisted.

"It won't be in a minute."

And the ache spread, deepened and quickened. Lizzie did not dawdle with the rest of her clothing. Neither, she observed, did Michael. She marveled at his body: all sleek and hard . . . and very ready.

"I've never known anyone like you," she said. "Never."

She opened her arms, and he came to her, kissing her everywhere. Images blurred, feelings, senses. There was heat, and white light, and colors, lots of colors, and melting. And throbbing. Everywhere, throbbing. She touched him intimately, and the throbbing was there, too . . . hot, primitive. The wet heat of his tongue was probing deep within her, knew he could feel her pleasure. She was absorbed by it, unable to think beyond that pulsing ache.

She was ready to scream out with it, and then he was moving on top of her, and into her, and she thrust upward, hard. He inhaled sharply, meeting her upward thrust with a driving, downward push that finally did make her cry out with pleasure. For a long time it was like that: thrusting, rocking, cries of sweet pleasure, and the blurring . . . the kaleidoscope of heat, light, and color, blending, blending, spinning, until there was nothing. No heat, no light, no color.

Slowly everything came into focus again. Collapsed, exhausted, Lizzie looked at Michael and smiled. "Hi," she said.

He laughed softly. "Hi."

After a while Michael offered Lizzie use of one of his robes. It was plaid wool and smelled of him. She wrapped up tightly. She wanted that smell in her life forever. He put on another robe, and they went into the kitchen where he had dinner all set to go in the refrigerator.

"Why do I have a feeling that this was planned?" she said slyly.

"Because you're a perceptive woman—and I'm an optimist. I figured something light would be in order."

There were melon slices wrapped in prosciutto, cold fruit soup, a vegetable salad, wine, and, for dessert, an obscenely delicious carrot cake.

"You'll spend the night?" Michael said.

"I don't know . . . Chelsea will worry."

"So? Call her. She's a big girl, she'll understand."

"Yes, but—"

"Afraid of what she'll say about you sleeping with that arrogant, nasty, wise-assed hometown boy?"

Lizzie laughed, "Of course not."

"Then call her."

Lizzie used the kitchen phone, but Chelsea was out. So Lizzie left a message for her roommate on their brand-new message machine. "Chels?" she said. "Don't wait up. I've been swept off my feet by a white-haired Wolfe."

She hung up, and Michael peered at her over the top of his wineglass. "So it's a Wolfe you want, hm?"

And it was a Wolfe she got, after dinner and twice during the night.

CHAPTER TEN

Under the cold glare of his desk lamp the following morning, Wolfe sat and wondered if he had made a serious mistake. Not in spending the night with Lizzie; his body was still suffused with the marvels of her. He felt energetic and languorous all at the same time, but most of all he felt the exquisite and indefinable power of love. Because he was in love with her. There was no question of that. The sexual tension was there—the physical attraction, the electricity—but undergirding it, strengthening it, was simple and pure love.

Wolfe had never been in love before, not like this. Before, he could always see the end of a romance even as it started—the flaws in each of them that would eventually break them apart. They would be too lazy, not committed enough to their relationship, to bother working at it. When problems started, one or the other would run. It was easier that way and much less painful.

But not this time, not with Lizzie. Wolfe couldn't

run, he couldn't take the easy way out. He was committed to Lizzie Olson. He was in love with her.

And that made his mistake that much more frightening. In the broad scheme of things it was a small deception: he simply had pretended not to have known all along who she really was. His motives were not entirely impure, but he didn't think any of this would hold water with lovely Lizzie. She would be, in a word, pissed. Wolfe would have to tread softly, but, because he cared, he would also have to admit his mistake.

Wolfe didn't like admitting his mistakes. He liked making them even less. He prided himself on his good judgment and foresight. But that was in business. This wasn't. This was romance, love, emotion, and all Wolfe had to rely on were his own very strong, very real feelings toward a beautiful and fascinating Kansas redhead. Judgment and foresight didn't amount to a damn.

There was a knock on his door. "Wolfe?" Meg Oakes said, pushing the door open. "I have to talk to you."

He pointed to a chair. "Sit."

"I know about Lizzie."

"Your husband has a big mouth."

"Chelsea told me too. Last night. We had her over to dinner, and she told me the whole raucous tale. It really would be funny except—well . . ." She hesitated. "Oh, hell, if you haven't killed me before now, I guess you won't kill me over this."

"Don't beat around the bush, Oakes. Out with it."

"I sort of let it slip to Chelsea that you knew who they were all along. I assumed they knew."

Wolfe glared at her. "*You* have a big mouth, Oakes."

161

"I know. I'm sorry."

"Forget it. What did Chelsea say?"

"She called you a cur."

Wolfe smiled. "I suppose I've been called worse."

"Michael . . . I know you care about Lizzie, and I should have kept my big mouth shut and not interfered, but I have a feeling Chelsea is going to tell Lizzie and—"

"*Of course* Chelsea is going to tell Lizzie. Those two have been sharing secrets since they were in diapers."

"I can talk to her if you want."

Wolfe shook his head. "No, Oakes, this time I'll do my own dirty work."

Lizzie knew Chelsea was hiding something and couldn't stand it. "Chelsea," she said, following her around the apartment, "you have to tell me."

"Tell you what?"

"Whatever it is you're not telling me."

Chelsea paused thoughtfully in the doorway to her room, which she had painted a pale blue, making it seem larger. "I think I'm going to have Mother send me out Granny's wedding-ring quilt, do the room in a contrast of country and city. It'll remind me of me."

"*Chelsea!*"

"Not in my ear, Lizzie."

"Who told you it was Albert Sorenson writing those anonymous love letters to you in seventh grade? Who warned you that your mother had found out about your wearing purple lipstick to the tenth-grade sock hop?"

"And I'll put Granny and Grandpa's picture there on the wall," Chelsea mused, pointing.

"Who *hired* you?"

Chelsea turned. "Oooh, that was low, Lizzie."

"I'm desperate."

"Why?"

Lizzie collapsed against the wall. "Because I love him, Chels." She looked at her best friend. "What you're not telling me is about him, isn't it?"

"Lizzie. . . ."

"You *have* to tell me."

"I can't."

"It's another woman."

"Don't be silly."

She nodded. "I know, I know. There couldn't be. He's not that sort. He's been married before and has five kids?"

Chelsea laughed. "You *are* desperate."

"How bad is it?"

"Not bad at all, really. I'm sure his motives are within the realm of understanding."

"His motives for *what*?"

"I can't tell you."

"Is it something someone told you?"

"Lizzie, I'm not going to tell you. You'll have to ask Michael."

"What, that my best friend knows some dark secret about him and won't tell me? He'll think I'm nuts!"

"He'll know exactly what you're talking about," Chelsea muttered.

"He's hired another designer. That's it, isn't it?"

"Oh, come on, Lizzie, you're not thinking clearly."

"If I guess, will you tell me?"

"Desperation doesn't become you. Why don't you get your tail down to Michael's office and hang him by the thumbs until he tells you himself."

"*Tells me what!*"

Chelsea went back into the hall and down to the kitchen. Lizzie followed. They both were still in their bathrobes, Lizzie having returned from Michael's apartment and taken a shower and a nap. Last night had afforded her little opportunity to sleep. Not that she minded. She was in love.

"Lizzie," Chelsea said, turning the gas on under the kettle, "you know I never interfere in your romances."

"Since when? I distinctly recall your telling me that Armand Godwin was a cocaine dealer."

"I never liked the guy."

"He was not a cocaine dealer."

"He wasn't a professor of medieval history, either, and that's what he told you, remember? He ran a sleazy clubhouse. Yuck."

"Nevertheless, Chelsea, you interfered."

"He wasn't right for you."

"And Michael is?"

"Yes, which is why I'm not going to interfere."

Lizzie sighed and tried to think up a new ploy, but the intercom buzzed, making them both jump. Chelsea got it.

"Who is it?" Lizzie called from the kitchen.

"It is, and I quote, 'Wolfe.' " Chelsea pulled on the tie to her robe and dashed back toward her room. "If

164

you don't mind, I am going to make an immediate exit."

Lizzie paced. Her heart pounded. Her hands were balled up into two tight fists. She began to perspire.

Michael was taking his sweet time about climbing the four flights of stairs. Was he coming to confess?

But confess what?

Last night had been so beautiful. So fulfilling and promising. Lizzie wanted that feeling of excitement and happiness to go on forever and ever. She wanted Michael to love her as much as she loved him.

There was a knock on the door. Lizzie checked through the peephole to be sure it was him and undid all the locks, tearing the door open. "Hi, what a surprise!"

He eyed her closely. "Chelsea told you, didn't she?"

Oh, dear God, Lizzie thought. "No."

Wolfe stepped past her into the living room. The sofa was still pulled out into a bed, but the room had been transformed from Jonathan McGavock's writing hovel. The walls were oyster-white, there were shutters on the windows, and the junk furniture was gone. Wolfe could see that Lizzie was in the early stages of working her miracles, but obviously she was turning this little place into her home. She was committed to staying in New York; there was no doubt of that now, not that there really ever had been.

Chelsea breezed out from her room. "Michael, hello and good-bye. Liz, I'll see you later." And she was out, gone, before either of them could say a word.

The kettle whistled. Lizzie went into the kitchen and

turned it off, offering Michael a cup of tea or instant coffee.

"Thanks, no."

He sounded so formal. She told him so.

"Lizzie. . . ."

"Chelsea didn't tell me anything, Michael. I know she's aware of something, but she wouldn't tell me." She whirled around, gripping the handle to the oven. "Michael, what is it? Please tell me. It can't be so bad as to erase everything that went on between us last night—"

"Good God, no," he interrupted. "At least I hope not. Lizzie, I recognized you."

She didn't have the slightest idea of what he meant and looked blank.

Michael rubbed his forehead as if he had a very bad headache. "I knew you were really Lizzie Olson the first day we met."

She stared. "You knew?"

"Yes. After we had dinner I called my mother and pried it out of her. I recognized your smile." He took a step toward her and gestured at the pots hanging on hooks above the stove. "You can throw something at me if you want."

"You knew," she repeated.

"I was caught between a rock and a hard place, Lizzie. On the one hand I had my mother telling me I damned well better be nice to you. On the other hand I didn't know what in hell you were up to and figured I'd better be cautious. And then I started to fall in love with you and really didn't know what to do."

Lizzie closed her eyes tightly. "I feel so *stupid*."

"Don't."

There was anguish in his voice, but Lizzie didn't hear it.

"Dressed up in that wig, the fingernails, the—and you there knowing all along." Hot tears squeaked out at the corners of her eyes. "Oh, God, I could die."

"I wish you'd thrown a pot at me," Michael said helplessly. He moved closer, reaching out. "Lizzie . . ."

She sensed his nearness and opened her eyes. The tears spilled out. "Just go, Michael," she pleaded. "Please, just go. *Please*."

"What difference does it make that I knew all along? Lizzie, I'm in love with you. I can't—"

"*Don't!*" She was sobbing now, furious with herself, humiliated. "You don't understand, Michael. I became Elisabeth Guest because I didn't *want* your help. I didn't want to be patronized. I wanted you to hire me because of my talent, not because you felt sorry for a girl from your hometown."

"I never felt sorry for you, Lizzie," Michael said softly.

She turned away from him so he couldn't see her tears, and so she couldn't see the anguish in his face. And the love. What difference did it make? He said he loved her. She knew she loved him. But what had their love grown out of? Deceit. Lies. Distrust. And pity. That was the worst part of it: the pity.

"You signed the contract practically without looking at it. You barely glanced at the space plans. And the laundromat—you knew that wasn't where I lived. You

167

let me lie and suffer from guilt about pretending to be someone I'm not while you laughed. And last night . . . *I don't need your pity!*"

Wolfe was rigid. "Do you want to give me the twenty thousand back?" he asked quietly. "Or maybe you just want me to forget last night even happened. Would that make you feel better? Well, I can't. I won't, damn it!"

"What I want," she choked out, "is for you to leave. Now."

And then he did exactly what she didn't want: He left.

Wolfe was not a patient man. Nor was he subtle. Lizzie Olson was an exasperating woman, but he loved her. He did not feel sorry for her. He never had. He did not waste pity on intelligent, capable women. And, not being patient or subtle, he had half a mind to stomp back up those four flights of stairs and tell her what for. Then they'd make love, and that would be that.

But this he did not do, because he did love Lizzie. She needed time to stew. To think things over and consider his point of view. After all, had he gone into a rage when she announced *her* duplicity? No. He had been quite chivalrous, actually. Of course, he could afford to be chivalrous: her duplicity was hardly news to him. His, however, was to her.

Which was splitting hairs, and he ought to bound up those damned stairs and tell her so!

No. *Be patient, my man*, he thought. *For once in your life, be subtle.*

He kicked open the door, stalked out to the street, and took a cab to meet an editor. With Lizzie on his mind he negotiated the meanest contract ever. It was going to set a record.

And he was going to give Lizzie all the time she needed to come to her senses. Unless she needed more than a day or two: Wolfe could bleed his reserves of patience and subtlety only so far.

Back at his office, he pulled out his contract with Manhattan Interiors. And there it was in black and white. His answer. He chuckled softly to himself: "Gotcha, sweet Lizzie," he muttered. "Gotcha."

Chelsea returned ten minutes after Michael left and found Lizzie collapsed in sobs on her bed. "Lizzie," Chelsea said, "you're a jerk."

"He knew all along!"

"No kidding and big deal!"

Lizzie sniffled and glared at her friend, who had planted herself on the arm of the couch, just above Lizzie's head. "Chelsea, you of all people should understand."

"I know: God forbid anyone should help Lizzie Olson. Like I said, you're a jerk. The man is in love with you."

"I don't like pity."

"Our Michael is not the type of man to lavish pity on anyone, least of all someone he *knew* was conning him."

"But he—"

"He was probably confused as hell. Little ol' Lizzie Olson of Wilson Creek turning up on his doorstep, dealing with his own ambivalence about Kansas, falling

169

in love with you. Damn it, Lizzie, you should be glad he knew all along! Because that means all those moves he made on your *were* to you, not to Elisabeth Guest." Chelsea sighed. "Dummy."

Lizzie sniffled. "You think I overreacted?"

"A tad, Lizzie, a tad."

"He left."

"Did you ask him to?"

"Well. . . ."

"You didn't give him the money back, did you?"

Lizzie shook her head, utterly miserable. She had never cried so hard or felt so foolish. Every time she thought about the torture Michael had put her through— she refused to think about the ecstasy—she wanted to roll up in a rug and stay there.

But what about the torture she had put him through? If he did indeed love her, he must have suffered, too, knowing what he did. Somehow, though, she couldn't feel sorry for him. Then she wondered; *Am I feeling sorry for myself? Do I want my own pity?*

"Thank God for small favors," Chelsea was muttering.

Lizzie pulled a wadded-up tissue out of her robe pocket and dried her eyes and blew her nose. When she was finished, Chelsea had a hand over her mouth, trembling. Lizzie glared at her. "Chelsea Barnard, are you laughing?"

Chelsea fell onto the bed, bumping into Lizzie, and let loose with loud peals of laughter. She held her stomach, "Oh, God, it hurts, I don't think I've ever laughed—"

"Chelsea!"

"Imagine what he thought when we turned up at that cocktail party with me in that damned red wig and you in the brunette wig with those fingernails . . . and, oh, I think I'm going to die laughing! Poor Michael, he probably thought we were material for the loony bin."

Lizzie huffed. "He should have told us then what he knew."

Chelsea quit laughing and propped her head up in one hand. "Then," she said, "you never would have fallen in love with him, and you'd both have gone through life wondering what might have been."

"We still might," Lizzie mumbled.

"Not unless you're a *complete* jerk."

"I don't know what to do, Chels. I-I'm scared. I've never felt this way before. If I make a mistake . . ." She swallowed, her throat tightening, more tears threatening. "What if he never wants to see me again?"

"Don't be maudlin, Liz. You've got twenty thousand dollars of the man's money sitting in your bank. Believe me, he'll want to see you again."

"Why, Chelsea," Lizzie said, feeling a smile come on, "of course! *That's it!*"

Chelsea raised her eyebrows. "Lizzie? You okay?"

"Never better. Chelsea, I have a plan."

For the remainder of Tuesday Lizzie and Chelsea stayed in the apartment and worked. On Wednesday Lizzie dressed up in Elisabeth Guest's designer suit and, having followed Chelsea's precise directions to Wall Street by public transportation, met with Laura Gold. Lizzie explained that she was newly arrived in

171

New York from Kansas, showed some of her designs from Wichita and Kansas City, and answered a lot of questions. Now, of course, she understood why Michael hadn't given Laura Elisabeth Guest's name, but that was all right. Lizzie was grateful: he had spared her a messy explanation. But he hadn't acted out of any misguided sense of pity for his interior designer.

In fact, now that she thought about it, at that point in their slightly unusual relationship Michael had probably kicked himself for being nice to a con artist. The more she put herself in his shoes, the more she understood how confused he must have been. Falling for a woman from his hometown who was parading around New York in a brunette wig and fake red fingernails!

She could laugh about it now, sort of. She wanted him there to laugh with her, but he didn't come to her and she didn't go to him. He had his pride, and she had hers—but that wasn't the point. It was, simply, that a Wednesday visit wasn't part of her plan. Neither was an apology. What if she went crawling back to Michael? *Please, Michael, forgive me for overreacting. . . . I love you, I ache for you at night, I understand that you didn't pity me . . . but pity me now.*

Yuck, she thought, she couldn't do it.

And Michael didn't exactly break her door down, either. She viewed this not as cause for alarm but for determination. Perseverance. She knew Michael Wolfe. He was a stubborn man: no matter the price he had to pay himself, he was going to give her plenty of time to be an ass. After all, she had asked *him* to leave. Of course, she hadn't thought he would. She had hoped that he would sweep her into his arms and make love to her there on the sofa bed. She would have swept him into her arms, but he'd left too soon . . . and it was best not to think about those things now. Concentrating was difficult enough as it was. And she did understand. Besides being a stubborn man, Michael was an honorable one.

Damn him.

In any case the interview went well with Laura Gold: She wanted Lizzie to draw up a contract.

On Thursday Lizzie drew up the contract, paid bills, toured art galleries in search of the right piece for Michael's office, which she didn't find, and wrote up purchase orders, which she didn't mail, for the furniture she planned to buy for his offices.

On Friday afternoon she called up Gwen Duprey at Wolfe Associates and said, "Mrs. Duprey, this is Lizzie Olson of Manhattan Interiors. Yes, I'm fine, how are you? Good. No, no, you don't need to put me through to Mr. Wolfe. Just tell him, if you would, that I won't be able to get the color board finished in time. That's right. I'll need at least another two weeks. No, make that three. Be sure to mention that because this is all his fault, I'll be billing him for the extra hours. It shouldn't come to more than a couple thousand. Have you got that, Mrs. Duprey? Good."

Exactly ninety seconds later Lizzie's phone rang. She picked it up on the eighth ring. Her hands were sweaty and her heart was pounding so hard it hurt, but she said coolly, "Manhattan Interiors, Lizzie Olson speaking."

173

"Get your butt down here," Michael Wolfe said. "Pronto."

"But Mr. Wolfe—"

"Or would you like me to come get you?"

An unexpected but delicious warmth spread through her at the thought. "An hour?"

"Thirty minutes."

She was there in forty-five. Gwen was not at her desk, and Lizzie sensed something peculiar about the reception area. Then she noticed: Gwen's phone lines were unplugged and her desk was neatened, as if she'd gone for the day. But it was only two o'clock. Michael's door was shut. Tiptoeing, Lizzie peered into each of the other four offices: empty, empty, empty, and empty.

She began to feel a tad uneasy.

Michael's door creaked open. Lizzie leapt backward in surprise, stifling a scream, but then she saw him leaning against the doorjamb in his tan cashmere sweater and dark brown pants, his white hair thick and tousled, his body as lean and strong as she remembered. It hadn't even been four days, but it might have been an eon since she had seen him. Nothing had changed. Nothing at all. She loved him now as much as ever.

"You startled me," she said, recovering. "I don't see anyone about. Is everyone out to lunch?"

"I sent them all home early."

"You did? Why?"

"It's Friday."

"That doesn't make any sense."

He smiled and folded his arms on his chest. "I know."

174

Lizzie wondered if she was being outfoxed. Or, more accurately, out-Wolfed. She hadn't counted on meeting Michael all alone. If she had wanted to do that, she'd have gone to his apartment, which she had scrupulously avoided because his apartment had that huge, gorgeous bed and all those spectacular memories and . . . that just wouldn't do. There were things to be straightened out, talking to be done. She had her *plan*, damn it! She couldn't be distracted by the possibilities of lovemaking.

But, of course, she was already being distracted.

And Michael seemed to have a plan of his own.

"Well, I suppose you can do as you please," she said lightly. "You're the boss."

"Hence the white hair." He unfolded his arms and gestured to his office. "Won't you come in?"

She sat on one of the wooden chairs and pulled it right up to the front of his desk, with the hope that he would go around and sit in his fake leather chair. Naturally he did nothing of the sort. He sat on the couch behind her, and so she had to turn her chair around face him. He had one arm stretched across the back of the couch, and she imagined herself sitting beside him, the back of her head brushing up against his arm. It amazed her that he hadn't commented on her attire: engineer pants, bright blue polka-dotted bandana, Wichita State sweatshirt, bright red boys' sneakers.

Then she noticed the ruthless look in his dark eyes and was amazed that he hadn't just gone on and lopped off her head.

"The color board is due Tuesday," he said. "Your contract states that one week after approval of the space plans you would submit a color board, which we would then discuss. I approved the space plans on Monday, but since it was in the evening, I'm giving you the benefit of the doubt."

She shrugged. "I'm going to need another two or three weeks."

This was an outright lie; the color board was completed. It was an interior designer's final presentation to a client and showed samples of fabrics and colors, pictures of furniture, and furnishings. From her first seconds in the offices of Wolfe Associates, Lizzie had started thinking about the color board. She had put the final pieces together during the last four days. What else had there been to do but work?

"Why?"

"Creative distractions."

She saw a trace of amusement in his eyes. "How creative?" he murmured.

"I mean, distractions to my creativity." She was flustered now, damn him. "Because of your lies."

He turned purple. "*My* lies!"

She nodded, calm. "Yes. They disturbed my concentration—so much so that I've changed my mind completely about the space plans, even. Since this is your responsibility, I'm going to have to charge you for the extra time I'll need—"

"Just try it, sweetheart."

"Trust, Michael. Trust is ever so important in a client-designer relationship. You violated that trust."

"And you didn't?"

She grinned at him dazzlingly. "Me?"

"Lizzie," he said huskily, "that's your second mistake."

"No, actually, it's probably my forty-zillionth mistake, all in all. I've made lots of mistakes. You see, I'm an interior designer. I know lots about architecture and building codes and color and design and what companies make the best rosewood desks with Italian marble tops. But the business side of my profession had been a struggle for me. That's probably why I went bankrupt the first time."

"Lizzie. . . ."

She looked at him. "I want to tell you, Michael. I have to."

"You don't have to—not for me."

"Then for me."

"Lizzie . . ."

She forced herself to interrupt and finish what she'd started. "It hasn't been easy to admit, not even to myself. I like to pretend it never happened. But the truth is, I was operating under a contract that didn't cover my interests adequately."

"Unlike the current one," Michael said dryly.

"I finally wised up and learned how to ask for help. This last one cost me. I worked for months on a deal with a construction firm in Kansas City. Then when the furniture came in, my client decided to refuse it. All the interior work was done, mind you. I thought I was covered: He'd approved the color board, the furniture wasn't defective, everything was fine . . . but, of course, it wasn't. He knew contracts better than I did. So I went back to the furniture company, but they knew contracts better than I did. They wouldn't take the furniture back. I had to eat every bit of it."

"Ouch."

"It was too big a loss. I couldn't handle it. Disaster, tears, the end. Talent is wonderful, but a little business savvy helps too. I took a couple of courses in business, hired a lawyer to draw up a contract with no loopholes, and came to New York." She looked at him. "I picked on you because you were so successful, and I wondered how many people like me you'd taken to the cleaners over the years. I figured you were sleazy and unscrupulous. They were things I *wanted* to believe, Michael, because they made my own mistakes seem less humiliating. I thought that for once I was being so damned smart . . . and then when I found out you'd known all along and were just being the kind and wonderful man you've always been, I was so ashamed."

"And angry," he put in softly.

She smiled. "A little of that too. I didn't want to be pitied. But my fear of being pitied has sometimes made me seem ungrateful. I'm not, Michael. I know what I've earned, and I know my strengths and weaknesses. But it's stupid—and cruel—not to thank people for help freely given. When I thought you believed I was Elisabeth Guest, I felt I'd earned the contract with Wolfe Associates, the referral to Laura Gold—just the chance to be in New York. Through craftiness, my own talents, it didn't matter how, I thought I'd earned everything. But then, when I found out you knew I was Lizzie Olson all along—"

"You thought you were a charity case."

178

"Yes," she said, "that's right."

Michael stretched out his legs, until his toes almost touched hers. "Of course, you wouldn't know how many times I cursed you to the rafters," he said. "You wouldn't know how many times I told myself I ought to put you on a plane and send you back to Kansas. How I searched my soul for every possible reason not to fall in love with an intriguing woman from my hometown. I was too damned dumb to realize that I was attracted to you *because* of our shared past, not in spite of it. Lizzie, believe me, it wasn't charity. It was confusion—and love." He smiled. "And is. Love, that is. I'm not confused."

Before he could finish, she was in his arms. He laughed and said her name over and over, and then his mouth was on hers and she was clinging to him, opening her lips to the heat of his tongue. His hands were on her waist, sliding down into her pants, cupping her buttocks.

"Michael . . . Meg and Gwen and the others, they're not coming back?"

"I made it clear that they'd be risking their lives, never mind their jobs, if they did."

"All bluster, Michael Wolfe."

He moved against her intimately. "Not quite, m'dear, not quite."

"Does that mean you planned this?"

"No more than you did, sweets. And this was Plan B. Plan A wasn't to go into operation until Tuesday."

"When I failed to deliver the color board on time?"

"Mm." His lips rolled against her, parting her thighs. "You'd have had hell to pay."

179

"Bluster, bluster . . . *oh*! Michael, do you know what that does to me?"

"I have a fair idea," he said wryly.

"Can we, Michael . . . here, I mean." She moaned softly answering his movement. "I don't think I can wait."

Grinning, he moved his hands up up her sides and under her breasts. "What about your allergies?" he murmured, unclasping her bra. "I would think naked skin against my vinyl couch would drive you wild."

"It would, I assure you," she said, inhaling sharply at the feel of his cool palms on her breasts. "But not because of any allergies . . . oh, Michael!"

He had lifted her sweatshirt and brought his mouth down to her exposed breasts, his tongue teasing, licking, circling one rosy nipple. He pulled the shirt off, and then came her pants, and his, and his shirt, and they were lying naked together on his tacky vinyl couch. Lizzie laughed, rolling on top of him.

"Who'd ever have thought," she said.

"Do you care?"

"Not a bit."

She arched above him and came down, easing him into her, slowly, until he, too, moaned. For a moment neither moved. "Michael . . . I do love you."

He answered with a deep, sensual thrust that erupted into another, and then another, until they were rocking together, pulsing, loving. And it was as it had been before and would be again and again: the heat, the light, the colors, the motion. Different and yet the same. And endless. As endless and permanent and forever as their love.

Then all was quiet again, and they were still, breathing hard but not moving. Lizzie shifted her position slightly. Something sparked inside her. "Michael?"

"Yes, love."

"I think . . . do you suppose we could do it again?"

He cocked a brow. "It'd be my pleasure, but are you sure?"

"Mm, yes. I—um—I think it's an allergic reaction."

He cocked the other brow.

"To the couch, to the couch, not you!"

But, nevertheless, he made her pay for her remark, and she was quite happy to oblige.

CHAPTER ELEVEN

Three blissful months later Lizzie was more in love than she had ever dared to hope was possible . . . and working harder than she ever had in her life. Manhattan Interiors was getting a reputation. Lizzie knew tomorrow night's opening of the new offices of Wolfe Associates would secure that reputation. Everything was done: the carpentry work had been performed to her exacting standards, the carpets were laid, the walls were painted, the furniture was in. Lizzie was satisfied.

Except for one thing: She still hadn't found the right piece of artwork for Michael's office.

"It's a case of knowing it when I see it," she explained to Chelsea and Meg Oakes over lunch.

"Well, you'd better see it soon," Chelsea warned. "You know, Michael. With him love is not blind. He knows damn well you've got three thousand of his money left over for 'art.' And he's going to want art."

Lizzie sniffed. "Have I ever cheated you?"

"No, fool that you are. Even those that deserved it—"

"I don't know," Meg interrupted cheerfully. "Wolfe's been saying his office looks a little 'sparse.' He's threatening to put the pewter sculpture back—"

Lizzie paled. "He wouldn't!"

"You must know our Mr. Wolfe by now," Meg said with a smile.

Lizzie did indeed. Every inch of him. He was there in her mind, always. But that didn't mean the man had any discernible taste for interior design. He *would* put that horrid pewter sculpture back, if it suited him. He had even balked at the new chair she'd gotten him and begged for his ratty old fake leather one back. Lizzie said sure, but she'd go back to her fake red fingernails. He had relented. The new chair, she promised, was scientifically designed, and after one day he wouldn't want to get out of it. This, he had said, he sincerely doubted—not with Lizzie in his life. Michael Wolfe had adopted a whole new attitude toward his leisure hours. He still hated Monday mornings, but for a very different reason: Weekends were wonderful and difficult to let go of.

"I'll think of something," Lizzie mumbled.

"What time is it . . . oh, gosh, I'm going to be late." Meg leapt up. "Catch my bill for me, won't you? I promised Wolfe I'd meet his parents at the airport."

"His parents?" Lizzie said.

"Mabel and Harold?" Chelsea said.

"Wolfe didn't tell you? Uh-oh, me and my big mouth. He invited them to the opening."

"Wait," Lizzie said, thinking. "Wait . . . *I've got it!*"

Chelsea sighed. "Got what, Liz?"

"The piece for Michael's office. Chels, how would you like to earn a quick three grand?"

Chelsea, being Chelsea, was willing to listen.

That evening Lizzie arrived at Michael's office early, before anyone else. It had been no easy feat putting him off. He had stopped by her apartment at three and suggested she bring her dress over to his place and change there. She pointed out that that gave her four hours to get ready. He said that he realized this. Her body began to tingle and ache in all the right places; she knew what he was suggesting. But she also knew what she had to do, and so she had called upon her considerable reserves of willpower and claimed she had butterflies in her stomach and had better just stay there and dress.

Michael had been less than cooperative. "Butterflies?" he scoffed. "You've never had a nervous second in your life, Lizzie Olson."

And then he had proceeded to show her just where butterflies would be located and how she would act if she had them, which, of course, was exactly how she *was* acting. She had mumbled something about Chelsea's being gone for the afternoon.

They hadn't bothered pulling out the sofa bed.

Now Lizzie was quite sure she *did* have butterflies in her stomach. Big ones with flapping wings. She pulled out her hammer and nail and set to work. Five minutes later the deed was done . . . and Michael was walking through the door.

"You weren't supposed to be here for another fifteen minutes," she told him, miffed.

184

He frowned at her. "I smelled a plot. What're you up to?"

"Me?" She shrugged, amazed that he hadn't noticed the painting on the wall behind her. But Michael's dark eyes were riveted on her, and she finally remembered that she was wearing a new evening dress. It was the sort of thing Elisabeth Guest would have worn, except in Lizzie Olson's colors. Quite striking and a tad sexy. She shook her head. "Nothing. Just a last-minute—"

"Wait a second." His eyes narrowed menacingly. "Move aside, woman. What in the name of hell . . ."

He stared at the painting. Lizzie's heart pounded.

"I don't believe it," he muttered.

He peered at the signature. "Chelsea Barnard." He glanced up at Lizzie. "You're kidding."

Lizzie shook her head.

Michael sighed, dumbfounded. Would those two women ever stop surprising him? That Chelsea could paint such a painting . . . and that Lizzie could know that it was exactly what he wanted for his office. He could look at it day in and day out. Four months ago he'd have paled at the thought. Now . . . now, with Lizzie in his life it was exactly what he wanted. The colors were muted and yet cheerful, the style primitive and yet nurtured, the mood of pride and yet humility, and hope. The subject itself was one Wolfe knew well: Wilson Creek, Kansas.

Specifically Wolfe's Paint and Wallpaper Supply Store. Chelsea had captured every nuance of the venerable old store, including Mabel Wolfe's flower garden in the side yard. Morning glories blossomed on a lattice.

"It'll need a new frame," Lizzie said tentatively. "Chelsea said she'd provide one."

"No, it's perfect." He pointed to the oak tree next to the garden. Chelsea had even painted in his tree house. "I built that when I was around eleven," he went on. "I used to sit up there and imagine all the places I would go, the things I would do."

"I used to do the same . . . after you'd gone." She smiled wistfully, remembering. "Of course, the wood was rotting then."

"They're good memories, aren't they, Lizzie?"

She took his hand and leaned against his shoulder. "Yes, good ones."

"What do you suppose your mother and my parents are going to say when they see this?"

Lizzie grinned. "That we should come home. But you needn't worry about my mother. The thought of New York City terrifies her."

"Does it?" His eyes twinkled mischievously. "My mother says your mother's having the time of her life."

"The time . . . Michael, what are you talking about?"

"If you can pay Chelsea Barnard three thousand dollars for a painting she probably never meant to sell, I can send Hazel Olson and my parents tickets to New York and put them up in a nice hotel and—"

"You mean, my mother's here!"

"For her daughter's New York debut. Of course. She said she wouldn't miss it, especially since I was paying. She's as—um—straightforward as I remember. Hildie and Jake paid their own way."

"They're here too!"

186

"How often do they get to see the opening for a fancy New York literary agency?"

"Michael!"

He grinned. "Full of surprises, huh? Figured I owed you a few."

"And you call me shameless."

"You are, m'love . . . in more ways than you think." He laughed huskily. "That, however, is not a complaint."

She kissed him. "I love you, you know."

"Yes," he said, "that's the other thing."

"The other thing?"

"I think our families agreed to come to find out about us. They're curious. You know, you never made any bones about despising me."

"I'm 'straightforward' like my mother."

"Mmm. What do you suppose we should tell them?"

"Well, if you're not ready to tell the people of Wilson Creek that you've taken up with one of their own . . ." She shrugged. "I'll understand. Truly I will."

"Like hell you'd understand." He put her hands on her waist and turned to face him. "And I'm ready. More than ready. But I don't want Wilson Creek to think I've 'taken up' with you."

"I don't understand. . . ."

"Don't you? Lizzie, I want them to know I love you. I want the whole damn world to know I love you. Does your mother still have her flower garden?"

"Of course. Roses, bachelor's buttons, morning glories—the works. Why?"

"Ever since I was a little kid, I've dreamed of being married in a proper Kansas flower garden. Like your mother's." He smiled tenderly, gathering Lizzie into his arms. "Marry me, Lizzie. Let me love you and live with you forever and ever."

She grinned, delirious with happiness. "Is that an order or a question? If it's an order—"

"Me order anyone about?"

"Not your style, I know," she said, tongue-in-cheek. "Which means it's a question, right? Lizzie, my beautiful, delectable, wonderful darling, will you marry me?"

"You can fill in another ten or twelve adjectives, if you like. Smart-ass, wisecracking, impertinent—"

"Yes."

"Yes what?"

"Yes, your beautiful, delectable, wonderful, smart-ass, wisecracking, impertinent love will marry you and live with you and love you forever and ever." She paused. "Except for one thing."

He frowned. "What's that?"

"My mother's flower garden usually peaks in the middle of July, which, if you'll look at your calendar, is but three weeks away."

"Then we'll have to announce our engagement tonight, won't we?" Michael said, grinning.

"Soemthing tells me that was your plan," Lizzie murmured, wrapping her arms around him. "I love you, Michael Wolfe."

They were still kissing when the Wolfes, the Terwilligers, Hazel Olson, and Chelsea Barnard arrived five minutes early.

"*That's* what I was trying to warn you about," Chelsea said.

Lizzie wasn't quite sure if she meant the painting or her and Michael.

"I see," said Hazel. "It certainly is a surprise."

Lizzie still wasn't sure.

"Perfect," said Mabel, "absolutely perfect."

"I couldn't have asked for more," said Harold.

"I never knew she had it in her," said Jake.

Michael evidently didn't share Lizzie's confusion. "A little overpriced, but I'm not complaining."

"Overpriced!" Hildie turned purple. "Michael Wolfe, someone should have cleaned your plow years ago."

"Hildie," Jake warned.

Lizzie giggled. Michael looked truly nonplussed. "I beg your pardon?" he said.

"My sister is not overpriced!"

"I was referring to the painting. I had no idea . . ." Michael glanced at Lizzie. "Is she always like this?"

Lizzie nodded. "Hot temper."

"I see. You don't suppose she'd 'clean my plow' at the wedding, do you?"

"Not if you minded your manners—"

"Wedding?" Hildie's brow furrowed; Lizzie thought her sister looked gorgeous. She was the kind of forthright, honest woman who was comfortable in any setting. "You mean . . ." She howled with laughter. "Lizzie, fifteen years ago, didn't I tell you Michael Wolfe was the man for you?"

Her sister grinned. "So you did, but he was obnoxious then."

"So, my love," said Michael, "were you."

"I know," Hildie said, beaming. "That's why I thought you two would make such a good pair!"

Michael laughed, and then Lizzie, and then everyone else, including Hildie, who didn't seem to mind at all that she hadn't yet said anything right. Finally she gave her sister a hug and started to cry. Then the caterer arrived, and the first of the guests; Hildie dried her eyes and, from what Lizzie could gather, had the time of her life.

But she did manage to keep her mouth shut and leave the wedding announcement to her future brother-in-law. Michael didn't mince words. He said he and Lizzie Olson were being married in his hometown of Wilson Creek, Kansas—"population seven hundred, give or take"—three weeks from Saturday. Then he held his glass of champagne up and smiled into Lizzie's eyes. They might have been alone. "To the love of my life," he said.

Lizzie smiled. "To the love of mine."

JAYNE CASTLE

excites and delights you with tales of adventure and romance

____TRADING SECRETS

Sabrina had wanted only a casual vacation fling with the rugged Matt. But the extraordinary pull between them made that impossible. So did her growing relationship with his son—and her daring attempt to save the boy's life.
19053-3-15 $3.50

____DOUBLE DEALING

Jayne Castle sweeps you into the corporate world of multimillion dollar real estate schemes and the very private world of executive lovers. Mixing business with pleasure, they made *passion* their bottom line.
12121-3-18 $3.95

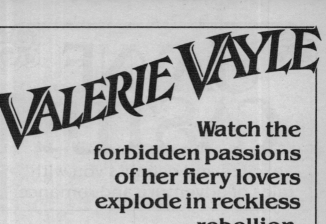